STRANDED

STRANDED

NIKKI SHANNON SMITH

SCHOLASTIC INC.

Copyright © 2024 by Nikki Shannon Smith

All rights reserved. Published by Scholastic Inc., *Publishers since 1920*. SCHOLASTIC and associated logos are trademarks and/or registered trademarks of Scholastic Inc.

The publisher does not have any control over and does not assume any responsibility for author or third-party websites or their content.

No part of this publication may be reproduced, stored in a retrieval system, or transmitted in any form or by any means, electronic, mechanical, photocopying, recording, or otherwise, without written permission of the publisher. For information regarding permission, write to Scholastic Inc., Attention: Permissions Department, 557 Broadway, New York, NY 10012.

This book is a work of fiction. Names, characters, places, and incidents are either the product of the author's imagination or are used fictitiously, and any resemblance to actual persons, living or dead, business establishments, events, or locales is entirely coincidental.

ISBN 978-1-339-01124-0

10 9 8 7 6 5 4 3 2 1   24 25 26 27 28

Printed in the U.S.A. 40

First printing 2024

Book design by Cassy Price

For the
Black Camp Fire Girls,
past and present,
of Oakland, CA

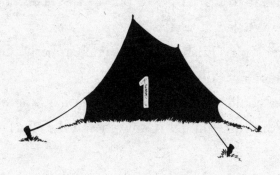

Walking into Central Park felt like coming home. No walls. No tall buildings. And no cars honking at you for crossing the street too slow. It was like Manhattan had disappeared. All I could see was grass, trees, water, birds, and blue sky. The only thing that made outside better was being on the big fifth-grade field trip with my three best friends on our second-to-last day of school.

"You guys, I can't believe we're about to be in middle school," Sienna said. Carlos's eyes bulged at the thought.

"I don't want to think about that yet," said Kimberly. "We're almost on *summer vacation*!" She gave Sienna a high five.

"*And* we're outside," I said, breathing it in. "You

guys want to walk over to one of the lakes? I read there are fish and turtles."

"Let's play Frisbee first," said Kimberly. Carlos and Sienna nodded.

We could play Frisbee anywhere. I wanted to check out the wildlife. "Can we go to the lake later?" I asked.

My friends nodded, so Frisbee it was.

The only one who could actually aim, throw, and catch was Kimberly. Sienna, Carlos, and I ran around on the grass laughing and fetching like dogs. When Carlos threw the Frisbee all the way into a grove of elm trees, I was glad. Maybe I would spot a bark beetle. They were spreading Dutch elm disease to some of the elm trees.

When I found the Frisbee, I didn't notice any beetles, but I did notice something in the dirt. I squatted down and inspected it.

"Look! An owl pellet!" I yelled, running back to the group with it cradled in my palm.

"It looks like poop," Kimberly said.

"That's nasty," said Sienna. "Throw it back in the woods and go clean your hands."

I rolled my eyes at them and said, "It's not poop. Owls eat, and then they cough up what they can't digest. It's bones and fur from the owl's prey. Isn't that cool?"

Carlos frowned and shook his head. I loved my friends, but they were definitely city folks. They would be totally out of place in the wilderness.

"You're so weird," said Kimberly. "Where's the Frisbee?"

"Weird? Why? Because I like nature as much as you like sports?" I crossed my arms and smirked at her.

"Okay, that's fair," she said. "BUT WHERE IS THE FRISBEE?"

I laughed. I was so excited about the pellet, I had forgotten the Frisbee, so I ran back to get it. I dropped the pellet and stared up into the branches of the elm tree. I could barely spot the owl, asleep on one of the highest branches. If I had brought my nature journal, I could have sat under the tree for hours watching and sketching.

"Ava!" Kimberly yelled. "You have to *throw* the Frisbee!"

I laughed, threw the Frisbee to Carlos, and watched it sail sideways over his head.

TOOT! TOOT! A double-toot on a teacher's whistle meant "come back to the meeting spot right now for lunch."

We ran back and waited for our teacher, Mr. Mack, to count us and make sure nobody was missing.

Sienna took a pink bedsheet out of her backpack and Kimberly helped her spread it out.

"Good idea," said Kimberly. "The grass makes me itch."

Even though the pink sheet was kind of extra, I was glad she brought it. There was one thing in nature I did not like: ants. They always showed up uninvited and ruined things.

We ate our sandwiches and traded cookies and chips while we talked about summer. Kimberly was going to four different sports camps. If you asked me, they weren't really camps, because they were at the high school. Camp meant being outside in the wilderness. I would never say that to Kimberly, though.

"I'm doing my own video series this summer," Sienna announced. "I'm going to read books and record myself doing reviews. Then I'll post them on my YouTube channel."

Kimberly was definitely going to be a big-time athlete someday, but I didn't know what Sienna would be. One time, she told me she was going to be an influencer.

"I'm calling this the Summer of Relaxation," Carlos said, looking proud of himself. "I'm playing video games, sleeping in, and watching TV. No activities. No people. No worries."

I didn't bother to tell them my plans, because I didn't have any. I didn't play sports, and I only played video games if I was at Carlos's house. I was *not* spending summer on the computer.

I would be stuck in our two-bedroom apartment with six people and lots of arguing over who sat on the toilet for too long. Mama would be working at the salon most of the day. My dad would spend his own summer vacation in chauffer mode instead of math-teacher mode. When we weren't taking Alex to his summer league basketball stuff, I'd be trying to hide on the top bunk so Arik and André couldn't bug me. A big brother was bad enough without the twins running around nonstop.

Summer was going to stink. The only way I was going to have any fun was to make a tent out of Sienna's pink sheet and pretend I was in the Adirondack Mountains like Auntie Raven.

Auntie Raven was my idol, even though I only saw her when she came to our house for Christmas. Her gifts were the best. Two years ago, she gave me a book about plants and animals of the Adirondacks. Last year, she gave me my very own mess kit with little pots, bowls, and silverware that nested into a carrying bag. And Auntie Raven didn't care what anyone said—she wanted to live alone in a cabin in the woods, and that's exactly what she did. What I didn't understand was why Mama never visited her own twin sister. They *were* total opposites, but that shouldn't stop Mama. I'd certainly visit if I could. It was probably nothing but fresh air, and blue sky, and all kinds of animals, and peace and quiet. I bet you could even hear owls hooting at night.

"You guys want to help me practice football?"

Kimberly said after we finished lunch. "I don't want to look like I don't know what I'm doing at camp."

"What about the lake?" I asked.

"Let's do that right after football," Kimberly said.

I shrugged, my friends nodded, and Kimberly got a football from the PE bag. "Okay," she said. "I'm going to pass it quarterback-style, so be ready."

Kimberly was strong, and every time she threw she had to yell, "Go long!" which meant the ball was about to go past you. If you wanted to catch it, you had to back up. A lot.

Carlos tripped over his own feet running backward and fell. I fumbled most of the passes. We laughed the whole time, but I kept wishing my friends were willing to explore with me the way they were willing to play sports for Kimberly.

The pass to Sienna was the farthest of all. Carlos and I watched as Kimberly launched the ball into the air. "Go long!" she yelled.

"I am!" Sienna yelled back. Her eye stayed on the ball, and she continued to back up—closer and closer to the lake.

I opened my mouth to warn her about how close

she was, but before I could say anything, *SPLASH!* Sienna sailed backward into the water.

Sienna screamed and bobbed up and down. "Help!"

The more Sienna thrashed around, the farther out she drifted.

"Try not to panic!" I yelled. "Can you swim?"

Sienna didn't answer. Kimberly, Carlos, and I ran to the edge of the lake.

"Somebody has to save her!" said Carlos as he took a step back from the edge.

"She's freaking out," I said, "and that's going to make things worse."

"Help!" Sienna screamed again.

"I'm not getting in that dirty water," said Kimberly.

Sienna disappeared under the surface and then bobbed up again. There was no time to worry about dirty water. I once saw a drowning boy get rescued from a lake on the news. I knew what to do.

"Go get Mr. Mack!" I yelled at my friends.

I splashed into the lake, then dove and swam toward Sienna. She grabbed my neck and her weight pushed me down. I pumped my legs to stay afloat.

"Sienna, try to get on my back!" I yelled. I turned my back toward her and pulled her arms to help her get behind me. As soon as she was back there, she wrapped her arms around my neck again. I pulled them off and put her hands on my shoulders, so she didn't choke me to death while I saved her life.

Once we were in position, I started to swim toward the shore. I couldn't believe my eyes. The entire fifth grade and the teachers were at the edge of the lake watching us.

Sienna was still in panic mode, which made her feel heavy, so I took a deep breath and put my face in the water. I kicked as hard as I could.

When I came up for air, I heard everyone chanting, "Ava! Ava!"

Finally, I felt the bottom of the lake. "Put your feet down, Sienna. You can stand up now."

We climbed out of the water into the crowd.

Sienna coughed and frowned down at her wet clothes. Kimberly ran to get the pink sheet so Sienna could wrap herself up in it.

"Are you okay?" asked Mr. Mack.

Sienna nodded and said, "Yes, thanks to Ava. She saved my life."

"You're a hero!" said Carlos. He grabbed my arm and raised it in the air like I was Muhammad Ali or something.

I smiled at him and thought to myself, *Not a hero . . . just Queen of the Wilderness*. Auntie Raven would be proud of me.

Mr. Mack made us sit on a bench in the sun to dry off. "Stay away from that lake," he said.

"You guys smell like a swamp," said Kimberly.

Sienna frowned at her. "I could have died in there."

If I hadn't gone in after Sienna, she actually might have drowned. She had totally panicked. She would never make it in the wilderness.

I would, though.

If I ever had a chance to *go* to the wilderness. And now I wanted to go more than ever.

I tried to imagine what my parents would do if I asked them if I could stay with Auntie Raven. It could be a simple no or a long-explanation no. Either way, it would be a no. Then I'd be stuck at home *and* mad at my parents.

But at least if I asked it would mean I had tried. I could do it at the dinner table. We always talked about important things at dinner.

Can I please stay with Auntie Raven this summer?

Would it be okay if I spend the summer with Auntie Raven?

Can I ask you a question? Is it okay if I go to the Adirondacks to stay with Auntie Raven this summer?

I was going to do it. And then I'd hold my breath and wait for their answer.

No.

Absolutely not.

There is no way you're going to live out in the middle of nowhere.

Hopefully, it wouldn't be worse than that.

Hopefully, I wouldn't cry.

Everyone was already home by the time I walked into our apartment. Daddy and Alex had a half-day at school, so Daddy had already picked up the twins from day care. I had completely forgotten that Mama was leaving the salon early so she could do my hair for graduation.

"Ava!" Arik yelled. He tackled my waist and gave me a big hug. I know I wasn't supposed to pick favorites, but Arik was my favorite brother. Whenever I read a nature book with lots of pictures, he climbed up to the top bunk bed with me so I could read it to him.

"How was your day?" Daddy asked.

Before I could answer him, Mama asked, "How was the field trip?"

"It was fine," I said. I hoped that answer satisfied them both because I was suddenly very nervous. All the time I had spent practicing my lines on the way home went out the window.

"Put your things down and set the table," Mama said. "Dinner is almost ready. We're eating early so I can start your hair."

My mouth went dry. I thought I had another hour before dinner and the I-want-to-spend-summer-with-Auntie Raven conversation. I nodded at Mama and did what she said. Everyone else jumped into action, too. Alex poured our drinks. Daddy took the twins to wash their hands so they would actually use soap, and Mama put a big bowl of spaghetti in the middle of the table.

As soon as we sat down, Alex started talking about his summer league basketball team.

"I can't wait to start," he said. "I'm about to be dunkin' on fools left and right." He did a dunking motion in his seat.

He probably *would* be dunking on people all summer, because he was good. Because he practiced all the time. Because he got to do what he loved every day, and nobody second-guessed it. Ever. Basketball wasn't *weird*.

But apparently loving nature was. Last summer, the Central Park Rangers had a lottery and the winners got to camp overnight in the park. I tried to get Mama and Daddy to enter, but they wouldn't. Mama said she wasn't sleeping outside. Daddy said we were better off "safe and sound" at home. Alex laughed at me and told me Black folks don't camp, which was a stupid thing to say, since our own aunt lived in the mountains. Auntie Raven was the one who gave me the nature journal.

"Ava," Daddy said, "you're a little quiet. Are you looking forward to summer?"

I wasn't expecting it to go down like this, with a direct question. I swallowed my spaghetti without chewing.

"No," I said.

Everyone but André stopped eating. André kept slurping up noodles. Mama, Daddy, Alex, and Arik stared at me. My parents looked concerned. Alex was smirking, even though he didn't know what I was going to say. Arik was curious, as usual.

It was like on TV when somebody slams on the brakes while they're driving—like this was an emergency. Or like there was an elephant in the middle of the road and nobody knew what to do about it. I had just halted dinner with one simple word. There was no backing up now.

"Honey, why not?" asked Mama.

"I don't want to spend summer in this apartment. Or in the gym watching Alex. I want to be outside." I took a breath and blurted out, "I want to stay with Auntie Raven this summer."

As soon as I said it, I wished I could take it back. It probably sounded a little rude, and it wasn't even a question. And based on my family's faces, it was a shocking thing to say.

"No. Absolutely not," said Mama. "There is no way you're going to live out in the middle of nowhere all summer."

My prediction was wrong. I got all three varieties of no. Not just one.

Alex started cracking up. "Something's wrong with you. You know in the movies Black people always die first in the wilderness, right?"

"Shut up," I said. Mama didn't like for us to say that, but right now I didn't care. If she had a better relationship with her twin, me asking might not be such a big deal in the first place. And maybe if I went, I could find a way to help them *and* myself.

"It's true!" He laughed again. "That's because we don't have any business out there. Black folks don't do nature."

"No." Daddy's voice sounded a little bit angry. "That's *not* why. It's because we don't get to star in enough movies. The stars don't die."

André slurped up more noodles. He wasn't paying attention at all.

Mama let out a big sigh. "Look, Raven made the decision to live in the wilderness alone. I don't know why. There aren't even any Black people up there. But that's *her* decision. It's no place for you."

There was a lot I wanted to say about that. First of all, I bet Auntie Raven didn't feel as alone as I did at home. Plus, Mama had never been to the Adirondacks, so how did she know who lived there? And I didn't ask to stay there forever. I just wanted to go for the summer. And after the field trip, I felt like I belonged in the wilderness with Auntie Raven more than I belonged at this dinner table.

I got that feeling in my eyes and nose I get when I'm about to cry. "Okay," I said.

"Well . . . let's talk about this," said Daddy.

Mama was wearing her poker face and nobody talked, so Daddy kept going. "For one thing, I'm tired of us setting limits on ourselves. Black people like nature, too. We can do whatever white people do. This ain't 1950."

Daddy only said *ain't* when he was mad. I didn't even realize how mad I was at Alex until I saw the look in Daddy's eyes. I felt the same way he did, and it was nice to have someone on my side for once.

Mama opened her mouth to say something, but Daddy didn't give her a chance.

He looked at Alex. "You ever heard of James Beckwourth?" Daddy asked.

"No," said Alex.

André scooped more spaghetti onto his plate.

"Who's that, Daddy?" asked Arik.

"He was a Black mountain man," Daddy said. Then he looked at Alex. "You have homework this summer. You can write a report on James Beckwourth and then tell your brothers all about him."

In a million years, I would have never expected this. I didn't feel like crying anymore. Even though I wasn't going to the mountains, having Daddy stick up for me felt good. I wanted to stick my tongue out at Alex, but I smirked at him instead. He glared at me and clenched his jaw.

"Ava, why do you want to spend summer with your auntie?" Daddy asked me.

Mama's eyes moved from Daddy to me. I hadn't practiced an answer for this, but I knew I had to say everything as fast as possible, in case it was my only chance.

"I love nature. I love animals and being outside. I've never been anywhere but the city. It's crowded and busy and polluted. You can't even see the stars at night, Daddy. I want to smell the fresh air, and live off of the land, and learn about the wilderness. I want to do something different," I said. "I want to have an adventure."

I left out the part about how he and Alex did everything together, and Arik and André had each other, and even though Mama should have been my person, she really wasn't.

"That's a little too much adventure," said Mama. "It's dangerous."

Daddy took a deep breath in and then let it out through his nose very slowly. Mama, Alex, and I watched him. I couldn't tell what he was thinking.

"I want to have an adventure, too!" yelled Arik.

"Here's what I think," said Daddy. "I think she should go."

"You think she should go?" asked Mama. She sounded half surprised and half like it was taking all of her effort not to lose it at the dinner table.

"You think I should go?" I grinned at Daddy.

"I do," he said. "New experiences are important. Passion is important. It doesn't matter if *we* like the wilderness. It matters that Ava thinks she does. Alex plays basketball because he loves it. Ava should have the chance to find out if she loves living out in nature."

Without thinking, I jumped up from my chair, scooting it back so hard that it fell over. I ran to Daddy and gave him a big hug. "Thank you, Daddy!"

"Don't thank me yet," said Daddy. "Your Mama has the last say."

Mama's voice was soft. "I love you, Ava. I don't want you to end up moving away like Auntie Raven did," she said. "But I also want to see you have fun."

That was not an answer. That was the opposite of an answer. It wasn't even a maybe. I didn't know what she was trying to say.

"Do you promise to write us a letter every week?" she asked.

I nodded.

"Okay," said Mama. "You can go. *If* it's okay with your auntie."

Daddy winked at me. This time I did cry. I hugged Mama. I knew she wanted to say no.

"Can I go with Ava?" asked Arik.

"No, son," said Daddy. "This is Ava's special trip. Maybe another time."

"I'll bring you back some pine cones," I said.

"And a baby bear?" he asked.

"No!" said Mama and Daddy at the same time.

I couldn't believe it. I was going to the Adirondack Mountains for the summer. I was going to be able to look up at the stars, sit around a campfire, swim in a lake, spot all kinds of wildlife . . . and hang out with Auntie Raven all by myself. I already knew she'd say yes.

I officially had the coolest summer plans ever.

"I hope this doesn't turn into one of those survival stories," Alex said with a laugh.

"Anyone can survive the city," I told him. "Cell phones, navigation apps, food for sale on every corner. It's dummy proof. I'll learn *all* the survival skills." I stuck my tongue out at him.

"We'll see," said Alex.

"You will see," I said, "because I'm about to show you."

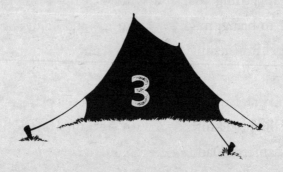

The next three days were a blur. It was like I had thrown my whole family into a state of chaos. Mama decided not to do my hair for graduation, because she wanted to do box braids before I left for *the wilderness*, which is what she kept calling Auntie Raven's cabin. She had gone from worrying about me getting attacked by a bear to worrying about my hair being in a protective style, especially now that it had grown down to the middle of my back. Arik begged nonstop to go with me, André wanted to know if he could sleep in the top bunk while I was gone, and Alex teased me whenever Daddy wasn't listening. I didn't care, though. On Sunday, they were driving me to the Adirondack Mountains, and nothing could ruin it.

Everything would be perfect. I had researched what to bring, made a list in my nature journal, and packed everything into two gigantic suitcases. I also put the most important things in my backpack, like the book from Auntie Raven, my journal, the mess kit, a flashlight, a knife, some weird, old-fashioned disposable cameras Daddy gave me, bug spray, and a few art supplies so I could make my journal sketches in color.

Right before we piled into the car for the four-hour drive to Adirondack Park, I checked my list one more time. Alex saw me and said, "You look a little nervous, Ava. You *scared*?"

"No." I made a face at him. "I'm *prepared*. It's called survival skills, but you wouldn't know anything about that, would you?"

Daddy put a hand on Alex's shoulder and squeezed it sort of hard. "That's enough," he said. "Get in the car."

Mama plugged her phone into the radio and played Beyoncé. I think she thought it would keep things upbeat, but it didn't. When the twins started to argue, she turned up the volume, and André snatched a book from Arik, who started crying.

"Stop crying and use your words," said Daddy.

Arik sniffled and said, "You're a dummy, André."

"That's not what Daddy meant," snapped Mama. "Apologize."

Arik apologized, and then Alex started up again.

"Ava, you're going to miss hamburgers and french fries and milkshakes," he said.

I shook my head. "I'll be fine." I refused to let him get to me.

"There's probably nothing to do up there, either. Does Auntie Raven even have a TV?" asked Alex.

I stared at him. "Who cares? Only somebody with no imagination would go to the mountains and sit in front of the TV."

He tried harder. "What if you get lost on a hike, or stuck under an avalanche, or ripped to shreds by a mountain lion?"

The only person he upset was Mama, who turned all the way around and glared at him. "Be quiet," she said between her teeth. Then she stared at him for a full minute before she faced forward again.

Daddy turned off the music and said, "Ava, what are you looking forward to the most?"

Right now, I was looking forward to getting out of this car and away from all of them, but I wasn't going to say that. The truth was, I was looking forward to everything about it.

"I don't know, Daddy," I said. "Just . . . being in nature."

He smiled at me through the rearview mirror and everyone got quiet. It stayed like that for a long time. The twins fell asleep holding hands. Alex put in his earbuds. Daddy turned on love songs and held Mama's hand. I watched through the window as the world seemed to spread out before my very eyes. Buildings got farther apart. Then they got smaller. When the trees outnumbered the cars, I smiled to myself, opened my backpack, and took out my journal. I looked out the window until I found a tree I wanted to draw and spent my time sketching and daydreaming.

I knew we were getting close when I saw a road sign for Glens Falls because I had studied an online map before we left. I cracked the window and let the fresh, warm summer breeze float in. The trees got even closer together, and I let

Manhattan disappear from my mind completely.

Finally, we passed a sign that said ENTERING ADIRONDACK PARK, and it was even better than I imagined. There was nothing but trees on both sides of a road that felt deserted compared to the city. It was like being in a different country. Even when we reached a small town, the trees and mountains seemed to stretch forever. I had done enough research to know that there were small towns and tourism spots in the park, but I hoped Auntie didn't live in one of those. There were sections of the Adirondacks where only one building every forty acres was allowed. And that's where I wanted to be.

Suddenly, a collection of modern-looking buildings appeared on both sides of the road. "The Outlets at Lake George?" asked Alex, laughing. "*A mall?* So much for the wilderness."

"Wow," said Mama. "They have a Coach and a Michael Kors store."

I had definitely not searched for shopping opportunities. I had no idea there was a plaza in Lake George. This wasn't what I expected at all.

"Look!" yelled Alex, who was obviously happy to see something other than what he knew I was hoping for. "Another one. Adirondack Outlet Mall."

"This is it," said Daddy. He slowed down and turned into the parking lot.

"Dad, can we stop at Under Armour?" asked Alex. "I need some new basketball shorts."

They were not turning my adventure into a shopping spree. They could do that anywhere. Why were we at the mall anyway? Daddy parked the car.

"Daddy, is this Auntie Raven's house?" yelled Arik, who was apparently now wide awake.

"No," said Mama. "We aren't going all the way to her house. We're meeting here."

That was weird. We drove all this way, and Mama didn't even want to see where I would be staying? "Why?" I asked.

"The Adirondacks are huge and Auntie Raven lives farther in," said Mama. "She offered to meet us here, so we can head to Syracuse. We're showing Alex around the college tomorrow."

I was relieved we weren't near Auntie Raven's house, but with all of Mama's concerns, I had figured she'd inspect the cabin top to bottom. I wondered if Auntie Raven did this on purpose. Maybe she didn't want to hear Mama's mouth about the cabin. I wouldn't blame her.

There was a knock on the back window of the car. We all turned around and there was Auntie Raven, smiling and waving. She and Mama were identical genetically, but everything else about them was different. Auntie Raven wore her hair in a buzz cut, and she always had on big, dangly earrings made out of nature. Today, they were wooden. Earrings were the only fancy thing about her. She never wore makeup, and her clothes looked like something a lumberjack would wear.

I was the first one out of the car. I ran to her and gave her a big hug. "Auntie Raven!"

She hugged me tighter than ever. "We are going to have a ball," she whispered in my ear. "I can't believe your mama let you come." She sounded as shocked and excited as I felt.

We both giggled, and she let go of me to hug my brothers. Then she hugged Daddy. Finally, she smiled at Mama and opened her arms. For a minute,

Mama just stood there, and I worried she was about to say something negative about *the wilderness*. But she burst into tears and hugged Auntie Raven.

I wasn't sure why she was crying, but I hoped it wouldn't get any more awkward than this.

They clung to each other like they hadn't been together in years, even though it had only been since Christmas. For the first time, I realized Mama didn't have a person at home, either. Even though Arik and André were different—and they *definitely* argued—they were best friends. It seemed like twins were *supposed* to have a weird connection. Mama and Auntie Raven obviously loved each other. Why couldn't they be best friends, too? We could share Auntie Raven.

When they let go, Auntie Raven said, "You okay?"

Mama wiped her cheeks with her sleeve and nodded. She glanced around at the little mall and sighed.

"I'm fine," said Mama softly. "The last part of the drive was beautiful. It is pretty here. You didn't have to move this far away, though. There are pretty places a lot closer than this."

It only took three minutes for Mama to start in on Auntie Raven. Even though she tried to sound all sweet about it, her funky attitude about *the wilderness* was right below the surface. This was exactly why she and her sister couldn't be best friends. Auntie Raven rolled her eyes and picked up Arik, who had wrapped his arms around her legs. Mama and Auntie Raven couldn't get along to save their lives.

Daddy came to the rescue. "Do you have big plans for your time together?"

"Definitely." Auntie Raven smiled. "We'll do some hiking, fishing, wildlife watching, and *a lot* of work."

Alex elbowed me and whispered, "You're about to be chopping down trees and eating fish eyeballs."

"You're about to be on my last nerve," I answered.

"Don't ever say goodbye on bad terms," Mama told us. She glanced at Auntie Raven when she said it.

"Are you still going to look at Syracuse?" asked Auntie Raven. She was probably as ready to get rid of them as I was.

Daddy nodded and opened the back of the car. My suitcases were in there, but there was also a gift bag I hadn't noticed. He handed it to me. "We put together a little something for you."

Inside was stationery and stamps from Mama, a lollipop from André, and an orange beanie from Alex. "So hunters don't accidentally shoot you," he said.

There was also something wrapped in a pillow-case. I started unwrapping it and Arik said, "That's from me. It's Pokey!"

Pokey was a porcupine, and Arik's favorite stuffed animal. "That's so nice, Arik. But won't you miss him?"

"Yes, but he's going to tell me everything when he gets back. You can sleep with him, too."

I hugged Arik, and the next thing I knew my entire family was standing in the mall parking lot, stuck together in a group hug. Even Alex hugged me.

Daddy helped us load my suitcases into the back of Auntie Raven's gigantic truck, and then it was time for them to go. Mama reminded me to write every week; Arik reminded me to kiss Pokey goodnight; André reminded me that if you licked a lollipop and didn't bite it, it would last longer; and Alex kept his mouth shut for once.

Before Daddy got back in the car, he took the whistle he used when he was timing Alex's drills off his key chain and handed it to me. "Just in case you need to make some noise," he said.

"Don't forget," said Mama with one leg still hanging out of the car, "email me at any time. I'll come get Ava. It's no problem at all." She sounded like she hoped that would happen, but if I had anything to say about it, it wouldn't.

Auntie Raven and I stood there and watched the car disappear back the way we came. Then she clapped and yelled, "Alright! Let's do this, Ava!"

We climbed in the truck and she rolled the windows down. "You have to smell it," she said.

As we headed deeper into the Adirondacks, I stuck my head out the window and inhaled the fresh air and the smell of trees. We drove along the shore of Lake George, and as I watched the sunlight dance on the water, I knew I would love every minute of my summer with Auntie Raven. She smiled at me, and

I was positive she was thinking the same thing.

The farther we went, the more it felt like a forest. There were oaks, cedars, and spruce trees. I recognized them from my book. I put my arm outside and let my hand ride up and down on the wind. I imagined it was my own branch blowing in the breeze. Above us, an eagle soared, and all of a sudden, I knew how birds must feel, because my spirit was soaring, too. I already felt like part of nature.

Eventually, the road got thinner, the trees got thicker, and little cabins and houses were scattered here and there. I was in the middle of the boreal forest in the Adirondacks.

The houses got farther and farther apart, and eventually we didn't see any at all. We continued for miles before we turned onto an unmarked road. We travelled dirt paths until I started wondering if maybe Auntie Raven had pitched a tent somewhere. Finally, a cabin came into view and the truck slowed down.

"Is this it?" I asked, hoping it was. The cabin was very small with a garden, a shed, and a porch with two old wooden chairs. The area right around the house had been cleared, but it was surrounded by pine trees. It looked like the kind of place you'd expect a little old man to live in all by himself. It was perfect.

"Yup!" she said. "Do you like it?"

"I love it," I whispered, taking it all in.

When Auntie Raven turned off the engine, I closed my eyes and listened to the birds and breathed with the pine trees. I wanted to remember this forever. When I finished my mental journal entry, I hopped out and ran to the garden. I didn't recognize everything growing there, but I noticed a planter labeled *herbs*. Then I ran to the cabin window and peeked in. There was a fireplace with a rocking chair next to it, a sofa with a bunch of bright green blankets and blue pillows on it, and a tiny kitchen. I turned and grinned at Auntie Raven, who was leaning against the truck watching me.

"Can we go in?" I asked.

"Let's get the stuff out of the truck," she said. "You have *a lot* of stuff."

At first, I was worried it was too much, but then she laughed. "That's good, because you won't have to do laundry as often. I do laundry by hand and hang it to dry over there." She pointed to a rope strung between two wooden posts.

"Do you hang your underwear out here?" I asked.

"No, I hang that inside!" she said, and we laughed.

We brought my bags to the porch. Then she handed me the key and told me to open the door. Everything inside was made out of wood. I thought just the outside was made of logs, but the inside walls were the other side of the same logs. The ceiling was made of wood, too, with beams that met in the middle at a point. The kitchen table was wooden, the two chairs were wooden, and the coffee table was made out of a polished piece of tree trunk. Her stove was the kind you had to light a fire inside of, and her refrigerator was half the size of ours. There was a short hallway leading away from the living room.

"What's back there?" I asked.

"Go see," she said.

I half skipped, half walked to a little bathroom and a bedroom. *One* bedroom, which was wooden, too, but Auntie Raven had decorated it with shades of orange, red, and purple. She had a million pillows on the bed and another rocking chair with a little footstool. The window looked out to the woods, and there was a little path leading somewhere. I couldn't wait to find out where. I also couldn't wait to find out where I was supposed to sleep.

"Auntie, are we sleeping together?" I asked.

She shook her head. "I'm giving you the bedroom. That way, you can have your own space, and I can tend to the fire and do what I need to do if you're asleep."

"I don't want to put you on the sofa," I said.

"It's a sofa bed. I used to sleep on it every night. I'll be fine," she said. "Well, put on your hiking boots. Let's hit the trail while we still have some light. Unless . . . are you hungry? Should we eat first?"

"Are you kidding?" I asked. "We can eat later. I'd rather hike!"

I dragged my suitcases to the bedroom and changed shoes. When I came back to the living room, Auntie Raven motioned toward a bookshelf in the corner near the table.

"By the way," she said, "I bought you some books."

I examined the bookshelf. There were animal

books, plant books, books about sustainable living, and a shelf of novels that looked like she'd read them each over and over again. The bottom shelf had three photo albums, and a handful of brand-new books.

On the wall next to the bookshelf was a huge, framed map that looked like somebody drew it by hand. At the bottom, someone had scribbled *20-Mile Map*. There was a square in the middle labeled *cabin*, which I assumed meant this cabin. The rest of the map showed the areas surrounding the cabin, including streams, trails, and natural landmarks, and one neighbor at the far side of the map.

"Auntie Raven, this map is really good. Who drew it?" I asked.

She laughed. "It's a long story. My professor drew that and tried to convince me to memorize it for my safety. But I don't need a map. I have knowledge and intuition."

I shrugged. "I like maps. I looked at one of the whole park online before I came here."

"Ava," she said, "before there were maps, there were no maps."

I smiled, because I didn't know what else to do.

If Auntie Raven wanted to go backward in time and live a simple, basic life, that was fine with me.

That was when I realized Alex had been right—there was no TV. As far as I could tell, there wasn't even a phone. But I didn't care. I opened the door and stepped onto the porch. Auntie Raven followed me out and sprayed so much bug spray on me I laughed. She even sprayed my boots.

"Can we follow the trail I saw from the bedroom?" I asked.

"Lead the way. And put this on," she said, plopping a hat with some kind of flap that hung over the back of my neck onto my head. "You don't want ticks."

I definitely did not want a tick. I straightened the hat and marched toward the path.

5

On the way around the cabin, we passed a grove of pine trees. I stopped to look up at one that towered above the rest, straight-spined and majestic. Two gray squirrels played tag in a spiral up the trunk toward the branches. High in the tree sat a bald eagle and above it was a blue sky shrouded by a few light gray clouds. I knew I'd have to draw this in my journal later.

This is where I belong, I thought before I continued toward the trail. It took us through a tunnel of trees and wound slightly uphill. It didn't lead anywhere specific, but we came to a small clearing with a toppled tree at one edge.

"Well," said Auntie Raven, "what do you think?"

"It's . . . magical." Without thinking, I put my

arms out to my sides, tilted my face to the sky, and twirled. Then I caught myself and stopped, waiting for Auntie Raven to laugh at me.

But she didn't. She smiled, nodded, and said, "Yes, it is. That's why I never left."

We sat on the tree trunk, and I knew now was the time to find out what really happened between her and Mama. "Auntie, how did you end up living here?"

She sighed. "I was in college at Cornell, studying environment and sustainability."

"Wait, Mama went there, too, right?"

She nodded and kept on. "I got to do experiential learning here with a small group of people. We stayed in the cabin, which was owned by our professor."

This just made me want to go to college even more. I couldn't imagine *this* being my classroom.

"When I got here, I realized how much I hated the city. I always had. It made me nervous—all those people, and sounds, and smells. I always wanted to just be at home. But here . . . the whole world feels like home," she said.

"That's how I feel!" I said.

"When my professor offered for me to stay here after I graduated, I never looked back," she said.

Now I knew why Mama was mad. She didn't hate the mountains. She didn't even hate Auntie Raven. She hated that her sister was gone. I remembered her words when I asked if I could come here for the summer. *I love you, Ava. I don't want you to end up moving away like Auntie Raven did.* Mama missed her sister . . . her *twin* . . .

Auntie Raven added, "Your Mama and I were supposed to get an apartment together after graduation, but I changed my mind. I don't think she'll ever forgive me."

We sat in the stillness for a while. The forest had as much sound as the city, but it didn't feel like noise. An insect buzzed past my ear. Birds chirped. Something tiny scuttled in the leaves on the ground, and the wind rustled the leaves in the treetops above us. It was like nature was singing.

"We need to head back now," said Auntie Raven. "We have to clean the fish."

"Clean the fish?"

My face must have given me away, because

Auntie Raven said, "There's no food delivery here. No pizza guy. You want to eat, don't you?"

I nodded and stood up. I was here for a reason: to live in nature. To leave the city behind. To prove I could survive here. To live a different life, at least for a couple of months.

I led the way back to the cabin and paused again at the tall tree. It looked like royalty. Like the Queen of Trees. After Auntie Raven passed me, I bowed my head, curtsied at the tree, and whispered, "Your Majesty."

This time, when I realized Auntie Raven was watching me, I wasn't embarrassed at all. This time, I knew I could be myself here. I wasn't weird, or nerdy, or not-quite-Black-enough. Here, I could just be Ava, Queen of the Wilderness, Sister to Her Majesty the Pine.

I worked hard to keep a straight face when Auntie Raven plopped a big, dead bass on top of a stone cutting board in the kitchen. Its eyeball stared at nothing. I liked fish, but I liked it better when Mama got it from the store, flipped it around in some flour and cornmeal, and deep-fried it.

"Auntie Raven, why don't you just buy your fish?" I asked.

"I respect the land," she said seriously. "Too many people don't care about anything but money. They take advantage of the environment. Humans are destroying the earth. That's not the footprint I'm trying to leave."

I nodded. Our class had studied some of the Native American tribes who originally inhabited this land. Auntie Raven was right; greed had destroyed everything.

"You have to learn to cook, Ava. The land will sustain you, but you have to know how to stay alive here," said Auntie Raven. After she looked me in the eye, she added, "You can watch and learn this time. Next time, *you* prep the fish."

I didn't look away one single time while Auntie Raven cut fillets off the fish. She used the sharpest knife I'd ever seen to cut a little opening behind the head, then along the back toward the tail. Midway down, she pushed the knife all the way through the other side of the fish and cut until she could pull away a section of meat. It wasn't even that bloody. Then she used her knife to take off the skin. She flipped the fish over and did it again. It looked pretty easy, actually, especially since it wasn't gross.

"Can we cook it outside?" I asked.

"Of course!" Auntie Raven smiled and rinsed off the fillets.

Then she handed them to me.

"Put them on the plate and season them with salt and pepper on both sides," she said. Then I followed her out to a fire pit on the side of the house near the shed. She taught me how to build a fire. We put a little pile of leaves and pine needles in the middle of the pit. Then we made a tent out of little sticks all the way around the pile. Auntie Raven lit the pile and waited for the sticks to catch and then added a few thicker sticks.

"Get two bigger sticks," she said, and pointed to a pile of wood under a tarp near the shed. "Lay them across the fire, but not *on* the fire. We don't want burnt fish."

She told me step-by-step how to cook the fish, and when I was finished, it smelled good. Like . . .

really good. I had obviously worked up an appetite.

We sat on the porch and ate our fish and a salad Auntie Raven had left over from yesterday. All the ingredients were from her garden. We sat and looked out at the scenery until it got dark outside. A mosquito kept buzzing in my ear, and I was about to suggest we go inside when I noticed something flickering in between the trees.

Fireflies. My first fireflies.

I held my breath and sat perfectly still. One would light up and disappear, then another would shine to the left or the right. Then a few would light up at the same time. It was hard to know where they'd light up next, so I had to look everywhere at once. It was so beautiful, tears filled my eyes. I had never felt like this in my whole entire life.

Finally, we headed inside, where Auntie Raven lit a lantern.

"Don't you have electricity?" I asked, still thinking about the fireflies.

"Sometimes." She laughed. "I keep a lantern lit until I go to bed, because it goes out a lot."

She lit a fire in the fireplace, and I sat next to it

and drew Her Majesty with the squirrels running up her trunk and the bald eagle keeping watch in her top branches. I didn't even try to draw the fireflies. Some things belonged in your spirit, not on paper.

Before I closed my journal I wrote, *June 16: The magic of fireflies lives here.* I wanted to make sure I didn't forget a single detail about the Adirondack Mountains and my temporary life with Auntie Raven. I already wished it never had to end.

I had always loved Auntie Raven, but being with her in the Adirondacks made me love her even more. When she came to visit us for Christmas, she never stayed more than two days. Mama always said it was *too cold* to do anything outside, so we watched movies and played games. I'd ask her about the Adirondacks, and she'd answer my questions until Mama gave her the side-eye. When she left, I always wished I saw her more than once a year—and that we could hang out alone. Even though I almost never saw her, I always felt close to her. Now that we were alone, I could see that she never was her whole, true self at our house. She and I were practically the same person.

On my second day, Auntie Raven grinned and

clapped her hands. "Well, what do you want to do while you're here?" she said.

"*Everything*," I said.

She laughed. "Okay, how about your top three things?"

As soon as my parents said I could spend the summer with Auntie Raven, I had written a list of exactly three things in my nature journal. "Go camping in the middle of the woods, swim in a real lake, and . . . join the Adirondack 46ers club!" I announced.

"Wow," said Auntie. "How do you know about the 46ers?"

"Research," I said proudly. "I want to start with Grace Peak. Did you know it was named after the first woman to climb all forty-six of the high peaks in the park?"

Auntie Raven nodded. "Yup. Being a member of the 46ers was one of my first goals when I moved here."

"Auntie!" I screamed. "Are you a member?"

She laughed and nodded. I officially had the coolest auntie in the world.

"I have to warn you, though. We might not get to all forty-six in one summer," she said.

"But we have over sixty days."

"We have other things to do, too," she explained. "Summer is my time to get ready for winter. I have to chop that fallen tree into firewood, repair the shed, and plant all my fall crops."

I remembered Alex's joke about chopping down trees. I should have known there would be work to do. How else would anyone survive in the wilderness? If I could help Auntie Raven get things done faster, we'd have plenty of time to do my top three things. After all, we had the whole summer.

I quickly learned that Auntie Raven *needed* to be outside. Inside, she seemed a little restless. She'd sit for a minute and then get up and do something unnecessary, like dust the bookshelf. If I suggested or asked about something related to outside, she would clap her hands and say, "Let's go!"

Over the next week, Auntie Raven gave me a *vacation orientation*. By the end of it all not only could I build a fire, clean and cook fish, and do laundry with a washboard, I could also identify all the plants in the garden and some of the edible wildflowers that grew nearby. I took a bunch of pictures with one of Daddy's old-school cameras, but Auntie Raven explained I wouldn't be able to actually see them until I got them *developed*, whatever that meant. She took me fishing twice, and even though I could put bait on the hook and cast my line, I hadn't caught anything. We hiked every day, and with the binoculars she loaned me, I was able to identify half the birds in the book she gave me in just the first week. I had also spotted deer, coyotes, and way off in the distance, a bobcat.

"You got lucky," Auntie Raven had said. "I don't usually see bobcats."

"I want to see a moose, too."

"They keep to themselves, but it's not unheard of."

I also discovered Her Majesty was both a queen and a castle. In addition to the bald eagle who perched there often and the playful squirrels, an army of ants lived under one of her large roots. I hated ants, but they were her small royal soldiers, so I stayed out of their path—which went way up her trunk.

On the seventh day, while we were having a

picnic at one of the higher points we had hiked to, Auntie Raven said, "I'm so happy you're here, Ava."

She looked like she was holding back tears. It never occurred to me that there was anything negative about living in the wilderness, but now I wondered if Auntie Raven was lonely. I hugged her and said, "I'm happy I'm here, too."

Her face shifted and she said, "Well, vacation orientation is over. We've got to get down to business. It's time you learn to hunt."

"Hunt?" Hunting had not even come close to entering my mind. "As in, killing animals?"

She nodded, and I could tell she was *not* playing.

"You hunt?" I asked.

She looked into my eyes and I made sure I didn't give her any reason to think I couldn't handle it. Even though I was positive I could not. "Yes," she said.

"With a gun?" I asked.

"God, no." She frowned. "I hate guns. Too many land in the wrong hands and get aimed at Black folks."

I let out a tiny bit of the breath I had been holding. "Do you use traps?"

"No, I don't want the animals to suffer."

"So . . . how do you hunt then?" I asked.

"Bow and arrow," she said. "And only in the winter if I'm snowed in and it becomes necessary to stay alive."

Bows and arrows weren't as bad as guns, but I still didn't want to hunt. "What do you kill?" I asked, even though I didn't want to hear the answer.

"Rabbits and squirrels, mostly. And sometimes birds." She never took her eyes off my face and I wished she would, because I was officially horrified.

I couldn't imagine killing a cute little squirrel, let alone eating one. I thought of my two little squirrel friends. What if she killed one of them? What if she made *me* kill one of them? I had two choices: kill an animal against my will or disappoint my auntie and fail at living in nature.

Then a third option presented itself. "Auntie, if you only hunt when food gets scarce, why would we hunt right now?"

She was quiet for a long time. Finally, she said, "Out here, it's good to know all the necessary survival skills, even if you don't think you'll need them.

Nature has a way of knocking you to your knees, and you have to be ready."

She stood up, packed our lunch containers back into her backpack, and said, "Let's go."

The whole way back, I dreaded hunting. I considered purposely missing the animal, but that was just another way of failing. I *could* just tell Auntie Raven it was against my beliefs. But that would sound stupid. It was like saying I was against staying alive if I ran out of food. I didn't know what to do.

Back at the cabin, Auntie Raven said she had a few things to do, and for me to relax. While she disappeared outside, I sat at the table with my journal. I took out my gray colored pencil and sketched a picture of the two squirrels. I realized they didn't have names, so I labeled them *Squarik* and *Squandré*, after my brothers. Then I laughed hysterically. My nerves were completely shattered. Now I'd really never be able to kill a squirrel.

Auntie Raven marched back into the cabin and said, "Alright, follow me."

She turned around and marched right back out,

so I had no choice but to follow her. "Where are we going?" I asked.

"You'll see," she promised.

We went back to the clearing with the fallen tree, where we sat on my first day. This time, it was set up as an archery field. There were three targets spread out in the clearing. They were literally paper bull's-eyes. One was stuck to a tree trunk, one was stuck to a bale of hay on the fallen tree, and a third was pinned to a scarecrow. An open case containing a bow and arrows waited next to the fallen tree.

Relief filled the spot in my stomach that had been threatening to give me diarrhea. "Auntie, where did you get all this stuff?" I asked.

"In the shed. You questioning killing something for practice made me remember the archery lessons Professor Young gave me when I was in college." She looked excited and I smiled at her.

"First," she said, "you need to strap this on your left arm." She strapped a leather thing to my forearm.

"What's this for?" I asked.

"It's an arm guard. So you don't hurt yourself

when the string of the bow snaps forward." Next, she took out the bow and an arrow. She did a demonstration of how to hold it, how to position and draw back the arrow, and how to aim.

When she released the arrow, it sailed to the tree and hit the center of the bull's-eye. She winked at me and handed it over.

I spent the next hour having the best lesson anyone had ever given me. But if I were being graded, I would have gotten an F. Auntie Raven was fetching my arrows from the bushes, tree limbs, and even a few from the ground six feet in front of me. We laughed the whole time. Finally, she told me we had to stop.

"Not until I hit a target," I said, taking aim.

I breathed, focused, and let my arrow fly. This time, it hit the corner of the paper. It didn't hit the bull's-eye, but it was close enough. I lowered the bow and winked at her this time. "*Now* we can go!"

That night after dinner, Auntie Raven pulled out a guitar. I laid by the fire and wrote a letter home while I listened to her play. After a short warm-up, she started to sing . . . and she was *good*. I almost laughed thinking about Alex's reaction to this particular scene. Black folks in the wilderness with folk music. I almost couldn't believe it myself. I drifted to sleep listening to a song about Winnie the Pooh and a house at Pooh Corner.

Auntie Raven was full of surprises. I couldn't wait to see what was next.

One day after breakfast, Auntie Raven said, "We need to go into town today."

"Why?" I asked. Auntie Raven usually stuck to a routine. Each morning after breakfast, we tended to the garden, dealt with any laundry or cleaning we needed to do, worked on chopping the fallen tree, made odd repairs, fished or prepped dinner, and then went on little excursions.

This was the first time we'd gone back into town. In fact, I hadn't even thought of going to town since I got here. On Fridays, we drove about three miles to the mailbox to check the mail and drop off my letters. We'd driven to a few spots to hike or see a waterfall, but we didn't get in the truck often. I'd much rather check something off my own to-do list for this summer.

It was already July and Auntie Raven hadn't mentioned camping or swimming, let alone taking me to Grace Peak yet. I was trying to be patient, but if we didn't start soon, I would have no chance at all of being a 46er. I halfway wondered if Auntie Raven had been here so long she had forgotten how to enjoy it. Sometimes she felt more like a tour guide than my aunt. Whenever I started feeling disappointed about it, I reminded myself it had only been two weeks. The last thing I wanted to do was get an attitude that reminded Auntie Raven of Mama.

"I need to go to the post office, and I need to go to the library to check my emails," she said. "I check them at least twice a month."

All of a sudden, I realized I had no idea what Auntie Raven did for a living. "Auntie, are you on vacation?"

"Vacation?" she asked.

"Yeah, from your job."

She got a look on her face that made me wonder if I should have minded my own business, then she said, "Sort of."

I didn't ask anything else, because I didn't want to upset her. I put on my boots and got in the truck. I made sure I took my graduation money with me, in case I saw anything I wanted—or in case I saw something Arik would like. I should probably bring back souvenirs.

About ten minutes into our silent drive, Auntie said, "I don't have a job. I'm surprised my sister never mentioned this."

Mama didn't really mention *anything* about Auntie Raven unless I brought up wishing I were like her, or it was almost time for her annual Christmas visit. I hoped I wasn't about to end up in the middle of some more sibling mess.

"I'm my own boss, and I take on odd jobs when I want to," she said. "Most of the time I stay here at the cabin and live off the land."

"How do you pay for your house?" I asked.

Auntie Raven let out a sigh that could have blown Her Majesty over. "I don't. Professor Young left it to me when he died."

My mind swirled with questions. *Was he her boyfriend? Why would a teacher leave their land to a student? Did Mama have a problem with that?*

"The short version is that he was divorced, had no kids, and outlived his siblings." She said it fast, like she just wanted to get it over with. "I took care of him here after he was diagnosed with cancer, and I had no idea he was leaving everything to me. He owned this parcel, plus the surrounding ones. The only change he made to the land was building a place to live. I've kept it just like he left it."

Auntie Raven's eyes were filled with sadness. "Do you miss him?" I asked.

She nodded. "He said I was the daughter he never had." She paused and added, "He was family."

I let that sink in. It seemed like Auntie Raven was closer to Professor Young than she was to her sister. I wasn't sure if that said more about Auntie Raven or about Mama, but it felt wrong. I couldn't see myself calling a teacher my family.

Professor Young had left Auntie Raven what was probably millions of dollars' worth of land. It was probably hundreds of acres, maybe even more. *That's why there are no neighbors for miles*, I thought. I wondered if Mama was jealous . . . or suspicious . . .

I remembered that when my Gramma died, they had inherited a lot of money from the sale of her house. Auntie Raven didn't have living expenses, a family to support, or college tuition to save for. Auntie Raven was rich—a rich Black woman who owned a big ole piece of land in the mountains and worked for herself *when she felt like it*. I didn't care what Mama thought about it. Auntie Raven had it made.

I spent the next thirty minutes staring out the window, trying to imagine being able to do whatever I wanted all day every day, and realizing that fixing whatever was wrong between Mama and Auntie Raven was going to be harder than I thought.

When we finally got to town, I realized how much I didn't miss people. Tourists were milling around in their white shorts and sun visors and sunglasses. There were way more cars than there had been just two weeks ago. It made me not want to shop for souvenirs. I didn't want to be like them.

"Why are there so many people?" I asked.

Auntie Raven rolled her eyes. "Fourth of July."

At the post office, Auntie picked up a package. The tiny library was near a tiny school. It was nothing compared to the New York Public Library, but it did have Internet. While Auntie Raven checked her email, I decided to check mine. I had exactly one email, and it was from Carlos. It said, *Hey, Homie! I miss playing video games with you. Summer is nice, though. I hope you like the wilderness. I hope you aren't dead from a bear attack. Write me back if you can. Do you have Internet?*

I wrote back to him. *Hey, Homie! I am dead from a bear attack, but I'm a ghost now and I'm answering this email. I'm at the library using the Internet. I love it here. I wish I could stay forever.*

On the way back from town, I got a fantastic idea. "Auntie, if I wanted to live with you for a year and go to school here, would you let me?"

She cracked up. "It doesn't matter what I'd do. *Yo' mama* would not have it."

"But would you?" I asked again. I couldn't get my mind off the little school near the library. Then I realized Auntie Raven lived here alone for a reason. I didn't know what it was, but maybe I shouldn't have asked to stay. I looked at her. She stared at the road ahead.

Finally, she said, "I would love everything about that."

Then, to my surprise, a single tear rolled down her cheek.

Poor Auntie Raven. She's really lonely, I thought. "Can I ask Mama in my next letter?"

She tightened her jaw. "Yes, you can. I'll add a little PS at the bottom, so she knows it's fine with me. But don't expect a yes, okay?"

I was sending another letter *tomorrow*. So far, I had sent her two, so she had to know how happy I was here. I had even drawn her pictures of the cabin, the trees, the clearing, and Her Majesty and the squirrels. She had to say yes. She *had* to.

Ten days later, while Auntie Raven and I were in the garden, I heard a car engine approaching. From what I could tell, nobody ever came up this far.

"Auntie Raven, are you expecting somebody?" I asked.

She stood up straight, put her hands on her hips,

and bent her body backward in a stretch. Then she frowned. "No, I'm not."

We stood together and stared in the direction of the road. Soon enough, we saw a silver SUV come around the bend. A *familiar* SUV. My heart sank. It was Mama.

Auntie Raven mumbled something I couldn't quite hear and marched toward the driveway. I followed her as my stomach twisted and turned. *What if my letter made her mad?* I thought. *What if she thinks I need to go home* now *because she doesn't want me to want to stay?* I worked hard to hold back tears.

We got to the car just as Mama was getting out. She threw her arms around me and squeezed me and kissed the top of my head about seven times. Then she let go and smoothed my braids. Finally, she smiled at Auntie Raven and said, "Hi."

They gave each other a quick hug before Auntie Raven said, "Hi. I'm surprised to see you." She sounded suspicious.

In my opinion, *surprised* was the understatement of the century. Shocked, dismayed, annoyed, terrified, confused, or full of dread would have been better choices.

Mama looked at me and said, "We got your letter. I wrote you back, but then I decided to come in person."

I couldn't read her face at all. The three of us just stood there in awkward silence until Auntie Raven said, "Well, since you finally ventured all the way out here, maybe Ava can show you around." Her voice was a mixture of sarcastic, happy, and hopeful.

"I'd love that," said Mama. And I could tell she meant it.

I grinned and showed Mama the cabin first. Then I showed her the garden and named each of the plants for her. I even showed her the meadow where I learned archery.

When we got back to the front of the cabin, she looked at her sister and said, "I don't think I've ever seen Ava this happy. She's so full of life." She had a sad little smile on her face.

She handed me an envelope she had in her purse. It was a letter addressed to me.

"Should I open it?" I asked.

Mama nodded.

Auntie Raven stood over me while I read it out loud.

Dear Ava,

I'm glad you're having so much fun. We can tell from your letters how much you love it. I loved reading about the fishing and the archery and the campfires. Raven used to sing to me at night and I loved it. Your artwork is beautiful. We all really miss you. Your brothers keep asking about you, and I can tell even Alex misses you. He reads your letters.

Daddy and I talked about your question. The idea of you not being here makes my heart ache. He called the school district and asked a few questions. They have a Virtual Learning Academy and a School of Independent Study. We would ship the school materials to you, and you'd mail back your work every two weeks. They would expect you to check in with the teachers, too. The credits and high school prerequisites will count.

I hate this, but we have decided to let you stay. But the rules don't change. Keep writing to us every week. And if your grades slip, you come back.

We all love you,

Mama

I jumped up and down and hugged Mama. "Thank you!" I shouted.

Then I hugged Auntie Raven. We rocked and squealed and giggled like two besties going to a concert. "I GET TO STAY!" I yelled over and over and over again.

When I let go of her, she was staring at Mama. "You remember me singing to you?" she asked in a soft voice.

"Of course," said Mama. "It's one of my favorite memories of us."

They hugged for a long time, and then we sat on the porch for a while. Mama filled us in on everything at home and Auntie Raven smiled the whole time. I knew it was because Mama was there. My mind was stuck on a single thought.

I was staying in the Adirondack Mountains with Auntie Raven for A YEAR.

Even though I knew I had a year to live out in nature, I still wanted to swim in a lake and go camping before summer ended. I didn't want to keep nagging Auntie Raven about it, because if she was more like Mama than I knew, she might give me a hard no for asking too many times.

But about a week later, the night temperature dropped cold enough that we didn't sit on the porch. Auntie Raven strummed on her guitar, and I sat by the bookshelf trying to decide if I wanted to read one of Auntie Raven's old favorite books or one of the new ones.

"Auntie?"

"Mm-hmm?" she said, still strumming her guitar.

"Is it going to stay this cold from now on?" I asked.

"No, it's still summer. Some days are colder than others, just like anywhere else," she said. "Why?"

"I was hoping we could go camping before it gets cold." I glanced back at her, but I couldn't see her face.

She stopped playing and looked at me. "Are you still in a hurry, even though you get to stay?"

I hoped the truth wouldn't sound stupid or whiny. "Well, I've been here a month. I'd like to check something off my list. I want to rough it. Learn to pitch a tent and be out in the elements. Honestly, I want to prove that I can survive anywhere."

Auntie nodded. "When I told your mama I was moving up here, she had all kinds of what ifs. *What if there's a blizzard? What if there are wild animals? What if you get snowed in and run out of food?*"

I could almost hear Mama's voice asking her those questions. I remembered Alex talking about Black folks dying first in the movies because we don't have any business being out here in the first place. Siblings could be brutal.

"So, can we?"

She smiled. "Alright. We'll go tomorrow."

"Tomorrow?" I grinned at her.

"We'll see if you're still grinning this time tomorrow!" She laughed. "Camping can be hard work."

The next morning after breakfast, Auntie Raven handed me a list. "Start packing."

I ran to the bedroom and came back with my suitcase. Auntie Raven frowned. "No, Ava. You can only take what you can fit in a backpack. One change of clothes. Extra socks, extra layers. You have to be able to carry your things with you no matter what happens."

I should have known that, I thought. I went back to the room and repacked. I made sure I had my knife, bug spray, whistle, flashlight, and mess kit. I stuck Pokey, my journal, and a camera in the outside pocket. Arik would be excited to hear that Pokey went camping.

This time when I came back, Auntie Raven had a *serious* backpack ready to go. We packed a second gigantic hiking backpack, with the words Mega

Mountain stitched on it, and put it in the truck, too. Then we were off.

"We're not going to one of the summer resort campgrounds," she said. "Since you said you want to rough it, we're going to the backcountry."

"Sounds good to me!" I said.

And she was not kidding. We drove until there were no other cars on the road, then went down one of the unmarked dirt roads that Auntie Raven loved so much, and finally she parked the truck. "Get the gear," she said.

Auntie Raven took her backpack and I took mine. She pointed at the hiking mega-backpack. "That one, too."

I took my backpack off, and she helped me put on the Mega Mountain one. It was almost as big as me. I held my own backpack by the strap on the top. We wound our way through the woods for about an hour and then stopped for lunch. I wasn't sure where we would end up, but we would definitely be roughing it. After we ate, we continued on for a while longer, and the backpacks started to feel heavy. I didn't complain, though. Finally, we stopped near a post with a little disk stuck to it that said CAMP HERE.

The spot Auntie Raven had chosen was perfect. It was just enough room for us, so there was no way other campers were going to stop here. It was surrounded by trees, so we had plenty of shade, and if it rained or got windy, we'd have some shelter from the weather. There was a stream off in the distance.

"The first thing we need to do is pitch our tent while the light is good," she said. "Then we need to make a fire pit and gather some wood. Once that's done, we'll light a fire and boil some water from the stream."

The only problem was that by *we*, Auntie Raven meant me. She sat on a rock and gave me directions for the things I didn't know how to do, but she didn't lift a single finger. I was already tired from the hike and backpack, and I was getting hungry, too. I thought about Alex and all his rude comments and how I had said, *you'll see*. I couldn't wait to tell him about all the things I learned how to do.

By the time I had followed all of Auntie Raven's

orders, it was dark enough under the trees that she had to put away her book. I put the lid on the water and set it aside. This was our extra drinking and cooking water if we needed it. Then Auntie Raven took out two potatoes, one ear of corn on the cob, two pieces of foil, and a cloth pouch.

It turned out I was cooking dinner, too. I made sleeves out of the foil and filled each one with cut-up potato, corn I cut off the cob, and some salt and pepper from the pouch. Those went on the fire while I unrolled our mats and sleeping bags. While I was working, I accidentally glanced at Auntie Raven and let out a big, frustrated sigh.

"Don't cut your eyes at me," she said, laughing. "YOU said you want to prove you can survive anywhere. So prove it."

I had finally found something Mama and Auntie Raven had in common. They did *not* play. And even though Auntie Raven wasn't wrong, she didn't have to be so literal about it.

I fixed my face and asked, "How long does the food have to cook?"

"You'll need to check on it in a little while, to see

if the potatoes are soft enough," she said. Then she lit a battery-powered lantern and set it on the rock she had been using as a seat.

I sat next to the fire and stared at the foil-wrapped bundles. When I thought they were ready, I opened one. Steam rose out of it, so I decided it was ready. I put one on my little mess kit plate for Auntie Raven. She grinned when she saw it but didn't say a word. She was a tough camping guide, but when I sat down and ate my food, I didn't care anymore. In my head, I checked a few more survival skills off my list. By the time I left, I'd know as much as Auntie Raven. Shoot, I would *be* Auntie Raven.

Auntie Raven handed me a canister after dinner.

"What's this for?" I asked.

"It's a bear-resistant canister," she said. "Put all the food garbage in it."

"There are bears out here?"

"Somewhere out here, yes. You'll need to store this away from the tent."

I checked twice that the canister was closed tight and walked far enough away from camp that it felt like I had gone at least two Manhattan blocks. I dug a hole with a stick, buried the canister, and stomped on the dirt to pack it down. Auntie hadn't told me to do all that, but I wasn't trying to wake up to a bear.

I wasn't sure what to do next. I watched the fire for a while, then I put my coat on, pulled the hood over my head, and laid on my back. Through the trees, the stars were brighter than any I had ever seen. It made everything else worth it. *This* was how I had imagined camping—just me and nature and peace and quiet. I stargazed until it was time to go to sleep, and we crawled into the tent.

In the middle of the night, something woke me up. Some kind of animal rustled outside the tent. Without thinking, I reached into my jacket pocket and grabbed the whistle Daddy gave me. I'd scare the mess out of whatever it was if I had to. It sounded too small to be a bear, but it seemed like it was circling around the tent. I thought I heard it sniffing. My heart pounded in my ears. *Maybe it's only a raccoon*, I thought. It moved away and just when I thought it was gone, it came back again.

I reached out to wake Auntie Raven up, but then changed my mind. I was supposed to be surviving on my own. And apparently, I'd also be protecting my aunt, because her instincts were not waking her up. Hopefully, we wouldn't both wake up dead. Since I couldn't see anything anyway, I closed my eyes. Supposedly, that helped you focus on your other senses. I laid there frozen until my muscles ached and whatever it was wandered away for good. Even after it left, I had to sing the Winnie the Pooh song in my head over and over again to calm myself down.

I was awake the rest of the night listening for creatures, but other than what I thought was a great horned owl, it was quiet. I wanted to go out and watch the sky since I couldn't sleep, but I had no idea what might be lurking outside of the tent. Instead, I listened to Auntie Raven snore, and watched the sun come up from inside a tent.

Maybe I wasn't Queen of the Wilderness after all. Being terrified all night probably disqualified me. I knew one thing—this was *not* a story I would tell when I got home. I could practically hear Alex laughing already.

9

The next morning, we boiled our water again and used it for oatmeal. Auntie kept staring at me and finally she said, "Ava, are you okay?"

"Yeah, why?" I asked.

"You look tired this morning."

I shrugged. "I'm fine."

"Well, you survived your first camping trip," she said. "And you did it mostly by yourself."

She was right. It didn't matter if I was scared. I did everything myself. If the creature outside had been vicious, I would have also probably saved Auntie Raven. I was more alert and aware than she was. I really was Queen of the Wilderness after all. If I had to do this again by myself, I could. I'd probably blow the whistle if something came creeping, though.

"So, when can we go swimming in a lake?" I asked.

"I don't know," she said. "Don't forget, we have to get all the winter prep done."

Auntie Raven didn't seem as excited about my list as I was. I didn't understand how anyone could live here and not spend the entire summer in a lake. There couldn't possibly be *that* much to do to get ready for winter. Besides, swimming in a lake literally took a couple of hours. How hard could it be to find two free hours?

We packed out everything we brought in and hiked back to the truck. We stopped in town before we went back home. First, we went to the post office. There was a box from home waiting for me, but I decided to open it at the cabin.

Then we stopped at the library to check emails. I had zero emails. Kimberly and Sienna were probably too busy to email me. I wondered what Carlos was doing. He was probably in some kind of video game trance. I guess Auntie Raven didn't have any emails either, because she got up when I did and headed toward the library door.

Back at the cabin, I opened the package from home. It was full of school supplies and textbooks. The fact that I was staying here for the whole school year finally felt real. My parents hadn't changed their minds. There was a smaller box inside the big one. It had a pack of flowered underwear and conditioner for my braids from Mama, artwork from the twins, trail mix from Daddy, and a paper menu from the Burger Joint from Alex. I rolled my eyes and then laughed. I shouldn't have expected anything different from him. I appreciated the gifts, though. Sending me things that would make life in the Adirondacks a bit better—instead of things that made me feel like they were judging me or feeling worried or sorry for me—was nice. I felt . . . loved.

"I guess I'm ready to be homeschooled!" I grinned at Auntie Raven, and she started giggling. Before I knew it, we were both laughing and hugging like Kimberly, Sienna, and I did the time we won the Burger Joint gift cards for being the top readers in third grade. Until now, I never knew your auntie could feel like your best friend.

Knowing I had the whole school year to stay with Auntie Raven changed everything. I didn't feel like I had to nag her about swimming in the lake or becoming a 46er. I knew she needed to get things done before winter, and I was glad I could help her.

We worked side by side for the rest of summer getting as many of the winter prep tasks done as we could. They weren't the most exciting activities in the world, but I knew I was learning what I needed to know to survive in the wilderness. We got the garden harvested, weeded, and planted for fall and we repaired weak boards along the garden fence. We put some kind of sealant around all the windows and bought wood to fix the shed. We chopped more of the fallen tree.

At least once a week after lunch, Auntie Raven took me on a field trip. The leaves had started changing colors, so we drove around looking at the trees. We visited museums and went on what Auntie Raven called *off the beaten path hikes*. She took me to a secret swimming hole near Shelving Rock Falls, which was a fifty-foot waterfall not too far from where my parents had dropped me off. We climbed a fire tower, and from the top, you could see lakes and the surrounding park. I loved every one of our field trips.

It started to feel like I actually lived in the Adirondacks, and I was just going about my normal business. Something about our routine was satisfying. Maybe it was knowing we were working hard. Or maybe I was just happy we were together. But every now and then, when the morning was extra cold, I remembered that summer was ending, and I still had things on my own to-do list.

Once school started, I juggled my assignments and all the chores Auntie Raven and I had to do. I was determined not to fall behind, and I made sure I kept writing letters home. I knew Mama was not playing when she gave me the conditions of my year with Auntie Raven. What I wasn't going to do was mess it up.

Middle school turned out to be hard, and it kept me from enjoying my disappearing fall days in the wilderness. When my science teacher assigned a big project, I wrote to Mama and let her know school had gotten busy, so I'd be writing less often. I explained that my project was due before Thanksgiving, and that my goal was to mail in all my assignments ahead of schedule. I hoped she understood that I was trying to do well in school *and* enjoy the Adirondacks *and* help Auntie Raven prepare for winter.

I had decided to do my project based on wildlife in the Adirondack Mountains. I used the idea of Professor Young's map on the wall, made my own map, and documented wildlife sightings, times, and dates. It was an excuse to get outside, go on hikes, and watch the land change. The Adirondack Park was full of yellows and reds I usually only saw in paintings, and the morning dew took longer to dry as the days passed. Every two weeks, we went to town, where Auntie and I checked emails and I mailed my homework to my study supervisor.

But the weather was cooling off fast. Finally, I said, "Auntie, I still want to swim in a lake."

"Yes, I think we need to go ahead and do that. I don't think we'll get the shed repaired, especially now that school has started," she said. "So, let's go tomorrow."

We went to a place called Nine Corner Lake. We had to hike there on a little trail along a mountain stream with tiny waterfalls. I focused on the birds chirping, the buzzing of insects, and the gurgling of the stream. I watched shadows dance on the ground as a breeze blew the leaves. I wanted to remember this magical moment forever.

"Ohhhh," I whispered when we got to the lake. "Auntie Raven, it's so clear."

"It's one of my favorite spots. I came here for the first time in college."

I waded into the water and just stood there, taking it all in. Then I swam toward the middle and treaded water. Auntie Raven stood at the water's edge smiling at me. I turned onto my back and floated with my ears under the water. I watched the sky and listened to the strange, muted sound of the lake. I adjusted my breathing, which sounded louder under the water, and tried to make it match my heartbeat. I closed my eyes and became the lake.

When my arms and legs were tired, I went back to Auntie Raven and gave her a big, wet hug. "Thank you," I whispered.

She didn't care that I was getting her all wet. She wrapped her arms around me and whispered back, "No, honey. Thank *you*."

I wasn't exactly sure what she was thanking me for, but I knew that being in the Adirondacks together had changed us both. We were each other's missing pieces. Together, we were whole.

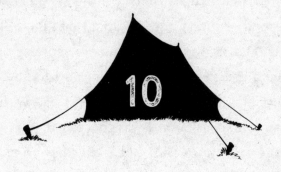

By the time the first week of October
ended, I had gotten way ahead in school—even in
math, which was my hardest class. Auntie Raven
was a math genius *and* a good teacher, so I started to
understand it. My work packet for our trip to town
was extra big, because the only thing I had left to
finish before Thanksgiving was my science project.
We mailed my work and headed to the library.

On the way, I said, "Auntie, can we hike our first
high peak next week, since I got ahead in school?"

"I don't know, Ava," she said. "There's really no
rush, and now that you have some spare time after
all, we should try to repair the shed. It'll only get
worse over the winter."

This wasn't the first time she made me feel like

what I wanted to do wasn't a priority. It wasn't even the second. I didn't say anything, but I was mad. Soon enough, it would be raining or snowing or icy, and she'd use that as an excuse. And I had worked my butt off in school to get ahead. I had earned a high peak hike, as far as I was concerned.

I checked my emails but didn't have any, so I wandered off to look at the books while Auntie Raven finished at the computer. She looked like she was concentrating.

She took so long at the computer, I finally went back to check on her. I was ready to go. I wanted to sit on the porch and sketch in my journal and enjoy nature, since it was obviously the only thing Auntie Raven had time to let me do.

When I got to the computer station, I saw that Auntie Raven was emailing Mama. I tried to read it over her shoulder, but I could only see the very top of the screen. She didn't even have Mama's email address right—the b in Robin was missing. I just rolled my eyes and went to sit in one of the soft reading chairs in the corner. Auntie Raven could proofread it herself.

When she found me in the corner, she had a

strange look on her face that I couldn't read. Her voice sounded tired when she said, "Okay, I'm done. Just one more stop."

The last stop shocked me. We went to a café and Auntie Raven bought me half a dozen cinnamon rolls to take home. I had to play it cool, like it was no big deal, but one of those cinnamon rolls didn't make it to the truck.

When we got back to the cabin, Auntie Raven said, "Ava, I need to talk to you about something."

This doesn't sound good, I thought. I hoped nobody had died.

"I got an email today," she said. "Something has come up."

"Please don't say Mama changed her mind."

"No," she paused and took a deep breath. "But you are going to need to go back home."

"WHAT?" I yelled. "Why?"

"I'm so, so sorry," said Auntie Raven.

"Did somebody die?" I asked.

She looked down at the floor like it was suddenly the most interesting thing in the world. "No. I have to go to California for a job."

I couldn't believe my ears. She was going to California for a *job*? She didn't even work. She didn't need money. Why would she ruin our plans like this? I couldn't even look at her. Now I knew how Mama must have felt. She was right. Auntie Raven did what Auntie Raven wanted to do.

"Ava?"

I didn't answer her. I had been taught to respect my elders, and I didn't know what might come out of my mouth if I opened it.

"Ava, look at me," she said.

When I did, tears rolled down my cheeks and I wiped them away with the back of my hand.

"I'm sorry," she said. "I really am."

I looked away again. "I thought you said you didn't have to work unless you wanted to. I thought you wanted me to stay." I thought about how she had burst into tears about it.

"This is different," she said.

She told me a long story about her friend Sophia from college who had been part of the group who stayed here that summer. Sophia moved to Lake Tahoe in California and did environmental work there. She had been in the middle of a big argument between the Visitors Bureau, the local government, and the locals, because tourism was impacting the wildlife and their habitat. The locals wanted new regulations to protect the environment, and Sophia was helping them by collecting data. But she was injured on the job and decided to get some optional back surgery, so she could be active and pain-free. And now she needed Auntie Raven to take over for her.

I didn't care. Not about California wildlife, not about Sophia's pain-free life, and not about Auntie Raven's stupid sense of responsibility for it. Where was her sense of responsibility for me? Where was her loyalty? Why wasn't her only niece visiting her for the first time ever the most important thing to her?

"Why can't it be someone else?" I asked.

"She trusts me. And she doesn't have family," explained Auntie Raven. "I'll work and also take care of her for a while."

"You've got to be kidding!" I yelled. "You're ruining everything. This is the most selfish thing I've ever heard. You care more about your friend than you do about me."

"Ava . . ." She tried to interrupt, but I was erupting.

"Well, guess what? I've been alone, too. I don't fit in at home, and this"—I waved my arms around in all directions—"feels like home. *FELT* like home. Obviously, it's not."

"But you have a family, Ava. She doesn't," said Auntie Raven softly. "She needs me."

So do I, I thought to myself. *This is exactly why Mama barely has a sister and I barely have an aunt.*

"You can come back for the second semester," said Auntie Raven. "I'll come for Christmas, like always, and bring you back with me."

When I didn't answer she said, "I promise I'll bring you back."

"When do I leave?" I asked.

"In a week," she said. "I already booked my flight and emailed your mama to come pick you up."

So, I was leaving in a week. And that was the end of that.

I knew better than to stomp off and slam a door,

so I held it together until I got into my room—which really wasn't my room at all. Especially since I was leaving it. I shut the door and threw myself on the bed. And I cried.

Everything was ruined. If Auntie Raven thought cinnamon rolls were going to fix this, she was wrong. She took the most exciting thing that had ever happened to me and made it the worst. I could already feel Manhattan creeping up on me, trying to smother me.

I don't know how long I stayed in the room with my face in the pillow, but Auntie Raven didn't come knocking. She knew she was wrong. I only came out because I smelled food.

Auntie Raven looked up when I came into the kitchen. She had the nerve to give me a little smile. "I cooked us some vegetable soup," she said.

"Thanks," I mumbled.

Auntie Raven sat at the table across from me. I could feel her staring at me while I stared into my soup. The last thing I was going to do was slurp it all up like I was grateful. Like everything was fine. Finally, she started eating, so I picked up my spoon and stirred my soup for a while. She wasn't getting off this easy.

"Ava," she said, "I can't just leave my friend alone while she has back surgery. And fighting for the environment is what I do."

No, but you can be quiet, I thought.

"Let's try to enjoy the time we have left," she suggested.

If she thought counting down the seven days until she sent me back home nine months early would be *enjoyable*, she wasn't as smart as I thought she was.

"Please?" She sounded like Arik when he begged to come with me. I looked up at her and was shocked to see tears in her eyes. "I don't want us to end up like . . ."

She wiped her eyes with her napkin. She didn't have to finish the sentence. I knew what she was going to say. She didn't want us to end up like her and Mama. Part of me wanted to tell her that maybe she shouldn't abandon me like she abandoned Mama. The other part didn't want to end up like them, either.

"We won't," I said. I hoped it wasn't a lie. But if I held a grudge, I'd be just like Mama.

"What would you like to do before you leave?"

I almost spit out my soup. I had literally just asked about it less than two hours ago. "Climb Grace Peak."

"I don't think we'll be able to swing that. I have a lot to get done," she said.

"What about me becoming a 46er?" I asked. I didn't even care how rude I sounded.

"You will. As soon as we get back and the snow melts."

I didn't know why we had to wait, but I was running out of fight, so I nodded and finished my soup.

⤴

I didn't stop being mad at Auntie Raven, but I started to understand. A little bit. The truth was, if Carlos was all alone and he needed me, I'd help him. Auntie Raven wasn't just leaving me, she was being a good friend. Plus, she was protecting nature while Sophia healed. Wasn't that what the Queen of the Wilderness would want someone to do? I didn't like it, and I was still a little salty, but what Auntie Raven was doing was part of what I admired about her.

I didn't bring the subject up again. I didn't complain or act disappointed. I didn't want to cause problems or make things worse between Auntie Raven and Mama.

But the magical feeling of the wilderness and being alone with my auntie was disappearing. I felt sad all the time.

The morning of October fifteenth was draped in the grayest sky I'd seen yet. Auntie Raven said something about a storm, but I wasn't listening. It didn't matter. Soon enough, I'd be back in Manhattan where everything was gray anyway, because it was made of concrete.

Auntie Raven's suitcase sat next to my things by the door. I wondered what they'd say if they could talk. Auntie Raven's luggage would probably be shocked because it thought she had forgotten all about it in the back of the shed. *I haven't left my dusty corner in years!* Mine would be confused. *Where are we going? We've never taken this many trips . . .*

At noon, we moved everything to the porch, locked the door, and sat on the porch to wait for my parents. I zipped up my coat, pulled on my hood, and hugged myself.

"I promise I'll bring you back after Christmas," said Auntie Raven for the thirty-ninth time.

I nodded and watched for the car.

When it still hadn't come an hour later, Auntie Raven started bouncing her right leg. I'd seen her do that when we'd been inside for too long and she needed to get outside. "Your mama was supposed to be here by now," she mumbled.

"Maybe they hit some traffic," I said.

Auntie Raven rolled her eyes. "Maybe she's trippin'."

I knew Mama was probably irritated about the change in plans, and making the drive *all the way to the wilderness*, but showing up this late wasn't her style. I wasn't sure why Auntie Raven would think she'd do that.

"She wouldn't do this on purpose," I said.

Auntie Raven snorted. "Yeah, right. Just like she wouldn't give me the silent treatment. She gave me the silent treatment when I decided to stay here, and she's giving it to me again now."

"What do you mean?"

"I *mean*," said Auntie Raven, "that she's mad at me for canceling your stay. That's probably why she's late. She's avoiding me. Silent treatment. That's how she is."

I didn't like being in the middle of their drama. At home, I had to deal with Mama, and now here I was still in the middle of it all the way up here in the mountains. They needed to get their act together and stop holding me hostage.

I was starting to realize they were both guilty. Mama was obviously holding a permanent grudge, and Auntie Raven seemed to have a habit of not prioritizing her own family. I could feel myself getting mad all over again.

Auntie Raven put her things in the truck and sat back down. "If I don't leave soon, I'll miss my plane."

"Maybe you should just go ahead and leave," I said.

She looked at me like she was considering it, then said, "I can't do that."

"Yes, you can. If I know how to camp in the woods overnight, I can certainly wait on the porch for a little while." I left out the fact that I didn't really want to see what happened if Mama got here so late that Auntie Raven missed her plane.

"You're right. They're probably stuck in traffic," she said. "But I don't feel right leaving you here."

For English class, I had learned about *irony*. And this was definitely ironic. She didn't feel right leaving me on the porch, but she was willing to roll out on my entire visit?

"I'll be fine," I promised. "Just go. Y'all don't need to see each other right now, anyway."

Auntie Raven nodded. "I'm sure they'll be here any minute. I'll probably pass them on the way down. She's probably thrilled you're coming home."

She handed me the key and told me to wait inside if I wanted, and to leave the key under the wooden loon statue on the porch when I left. She gave me a hug so long and tight it felt guilty, and off she went. I watched the truck round the bend and returned to my chair on the porch. Soon enough, I'd be leaving Adirondack Park, too.

I tried to be excited about seeing Sienna, Kimberly, and Carlos again. I tried to be curious about middle school and having seven different teachers and meeting new people. I tried to be happy about seeing the twins again, especially Arik. I tried to be excited about going to the Burger Joint again. But I was none of those things.

I only realized how much time had passed when it got dark enough to signal evening. I walked down to where the road curved, realized it was dumb to go any farther at dusk, and came back. Maybe traffic was worse than they expected. Maybe there was a wreck on the freeway. Maybe Alex had a game, and it ran behind or went into overtime. *But overtime isn't six hours.*

Whatever happened, it wasn't helping me feel any better about leaving the Adirondacks. Auntie Raven deserted me, and it seemed like my own parents didn't care enough to be on time to take me home. I went back inside to wait, taking my bags in with me. I might as well enjoy the extra time. Even though I didn't have a clue how to play, I picked up Auntie Raven's guitar and made up a song about not wanting to go home. I walked into the bedroom to look around one more time. I read a book for ten minutes and put it back on the shelf.

At 8:00, I stood at the window. Something was wrong. This wasn't like them at all. I hoped they hadn't gotten in an accident. They wouldn't have any way to let me know they were running late. They wouldn't have any way to let Auntie Raven know someone should come check on me, either. There was nothing I could do but wait.

At 9:00, I locked the door and lit a fire. If they showed up tonight, we'd all need to spend the night anyway. I might as well warm it up. I alternated between looking out the window, watching the fire, worrying, and being glad I was still in the mountains. When I got hungry, I ate the trail mix Daddy had sent.

Two hours later, I could barely keep my eyes open. I put another piece of wood on the fire and laid on the sofa. I covered myself with a bunch of blankets, hugged Pokey, and sang Auntie Raven's song about Winnie the Pooh. I was suddenly positive my family wasn't coming tonight. There was no way they'd try to make their way up here this late. I should have known that as soon as it got dark.

"Maybe they'll just leave me here," I said out loud. Then I laughed, even though it wasn't funny.

12

Somehow, I slept through the night, which meant one thing: My family hadn't come to get me. I sat on the sofa trying to figure out what to do. I literally had no means of communication at all, so there weren't a lot of choices. The only one that might work meant walking to the nearest house. If the scale of the 20-Mile Map was accurate, the nearest house was about ten miles away and in the opposite direction from where Daddy would be driving. If I left and they showed up, they wouldn't pass me on the way. They'd knock on the door, get no answer, and then who knows what would happen. And town wasn't even *on* the map.

I couldn't think of a single good reason why they wouldn't be here yet. The more I thought, the worse the reasons became. There was no way traffic was *this* bad. If they'd had a small accident, they still would have gotten here by now. Maybe they were hospitalized. Or dead.

I shoved my thoughts to the side and thought about food. Auntie Raven had cleaned out any food that might spoil, so the first thing I did was check the cabinets and refrigerator. There were two fish in the freezer plus whatever was left to harvest in the garden. Being an environmentalist meant that Auntie Raven didn't believe in buying canned food with a bunch of preservatives in it. I did find a sack of dried red beans and a bag of rice, though. It was enough for a week of dinners if I stretched it out. There was plenty of oatmeal, so that's what I ate for breakfast.

"Okay, Ava," I said to myself. "What are we going to do about this?"

I didn't know the answer, so I put on my coat and sat on the porch chair to think about it. I decided it was too early to start talking to myself, so I didn't do it again.

I wished I could go on a hike or go bird watching,

but I was afraid to leave the cabin. I went to visit Her Majesty. "I'll miss you," I said. "I'm leaving for a while, but I'll be back. I know you'll take care of things until then."

Squarik and Squandré were nowhere to be found. The ants were marching single file up the tree and back down again. Some of them were carrying white specks on their backs. A beetle crawled over the roots like a tiny ATV. I gave Her Majesty a hug on the side with no ants.

Next, I wandered to the garden. A few weeds had popped up since Auntie Raven and I last cleared it, so I pulled them and put them in the compost bin. Then I sat on the porch again.

Ten minutes later, I brought my journal outside. Instead of drawing I wrote, *October 16: I'm stranded at the cabin. I wonder where my family is.*

Then my brain completely switched, and I wondered if they were doing this on purpose. What if they were teaching me a lesson by making me wait? Not one of them thought I should have come up here. I had complained about summer and promised to show them just how capable I was. Now they were teaching me a lesson. They were going to make me wait a day or two.

Then my heart sank. Mama was giving Auntie Raven the silent treatment for at least the second time. What if she was mad at me, too? After all, I left just like Auntie Raven did, and I didn't want to come back. We were the same. I wasn't even positive she liked her sister. What if Mama was holding a grudge against *me*? The idea of my own mother feeling that way about me almost made me cry. But then I got mad.

Well, I'd show them. I would be fine for a day or two. I'd be fine for a *year*. I didn't want to go home anyway.

With a new sense of purpose, I marched out to the wood pile and took a bunch of wood into the cabin. Then, since it was breezy and still gray outside, I re-covered the wood pile with the tarp and put rocks on it to hold it down.

I put my suitcases in the bedroom, unpacked my school box again, and turned the table back into a desk. I'd show my parents I had what it took to take care of myself and get my schoolwork done, too.

That way, after Christmas, they wouldn't have a reason to tell me I couldn't come back.

Next, I washed my underwear, jeans, and two long-sleeved shirts and hung them over the porch chairs to dry so they wouldn't get rained on. I didn't care that I had flowered underwear all over the place. There was nobody to see them.

By the time I had done all this, it was time to fix dinner. I wouldn't thaw out the fish, because I didn't want to waste it if my family showed up. I'd never made red beans and rice, but I'd eaten it hundreds of times . . . with fried fish. My stomach growled. I wasn't sure what Mama put in them to make them so good, but I probably didn't have whatever it was anyway. I threw the beans in some water with salt, pepper, and herbs from a pouch that literally said *dried herbs* on it.

My dinner wasn't nasty, but it wasn't good. Tomorrow, I'd cook a fish. That way, when my family showed up, they'd find me eating a home-cooked, balanced meal. Even though they were jerks for what they were doing, I'd let them taste it, just to show off. The Queen of the Wilderness was unfazed.

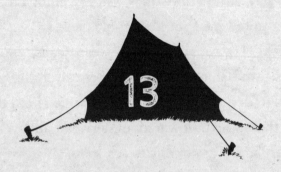

I cooked my fish and ate half of it with leftover beans and rice, but my parents didn't come. They didn't come the next day or the thirteen days that followed.

Now that it had been two weeks, dread was creeping in again. No matter how mad Mama might be, she also thought living in the wilderness was *dangerous*. She would never leave me alone for this long. Would she? I was pretty sure Daddy wouldn't let her anyway. That is, if Daddy knew. He thought Mama and Auntie Raven were *childish*. I didn't think Mama would keep a secret from him, but there was obviously a lot I didn't know.

I was sick of oatmeal and beans and rice. The thought of more fish made me want to vomit. I was sick of being alone and staying close to the cabin. How had Auntie Raven done this for years? Cabin fever was a real thing. I was actually glad I had my project to keep me busy. My journal wasn't even a nature journal anymore. I drew a picture of the twins. Then I drew a picture of Alex dunking. Finally, I wrote, *October 30: I've been here by myself for two weeks. Tomorrow is Halloween. I wonder if my friends are dressing up? The days are getting shorter and it's colder outside. Something bad has happened. Maybe. I don't know. I think I need to do the rest of the winter prep Auntie said we would do together. I think I need a plan.*

My mind wouldn't focus, though. It jumped from wanting to go home to not. From death and destruction to grudges. One thing didn't change, though. I was getting lonely. I got a piece of stationery and wrote a letter that I knew I couldn't send.

Dear Mama and Daddy,

I've been by myself for two weeks. I don't know why you aren't here. I'm a little worried, but I'm fine. I have firewood and am safe inside. I'm trying out new recipes while I wait for you. I taught myself how to make beans and rice. Maybe when you come, I can cook you some.

Love, Ava

I wished there was a way for them to know that I wanted to cook for them. That I loved them. Then it hit me. I had Auntie Raven's keys. I had the mail key! I could mail my letter and I could check the mail. Maybe there was something useful in the mailbox. And maybe there was a letter from home. My elementary school was about two miles from our apartment, and it took me about forty minutes if I walked. That meant it would take about an hour to get to the mailbox. *And an hour to get back.* It was a long walk, but if there was something good in the mail, it would be worth it.

I got one of Auntie Raven's raggedy-looking sweaters and one of the new books she bought for me. I figured a new book wouldn't have any special value to her. I hung the sweater on the back of one of the porch chairs and left the book on the seat to make it look like someone was home. I'd leave them there from now on. If my parents came while I was out, they would assume I was somewhere nearby and wait instead of turning around and leaving.

I smiled and headed to the mailbox. I should have thought of this sooner. I stayed off the road, because I didn't want anybody stopping and asking me a bunch of questions or offering me a ride or getting in my business—even though we never saw people on this road, anyway. It felt good to get away from the cabin, and I wasn't even that tired when I got to the mailbox.

I opened it and said, "Yessss!" There was mail. Three things, in fact. The first envelope was a letter from the 46ers for Auntie Raven. Next was a letter from home. I ripped it open.

Dear Ava,

We miss you so much. We miss your letters, too, but we're so proud of you for focusing on your schoolwork. It sounds like you're learning a lot and having fun. The twins like kindergarten, and Alex is ready for basketball season to start. We can't wait to see you on Christmas and hear all about your experiences.

Love, Mama

"This doesn't make sense," I said out loud. "Christmas?"

I looked at the top of the letter. It was dated October 11. *Over two weeks ago.* I felt dizzy. My family wasn't in an accident. They were never planning to come get me at all. They were just leaving me here and acting like it was no big deal. At least Mama didn't seem like she was mad at me, but why would they do this? I reread the letter.

I shook my head. "I don't believe this."

I looked at the third piece of mail, which turned out not to be mail at all. It was a postcard that said *Mail Hold: October 15–January 1.* Auntie had stopped the mail while she was gone. Mama's letter must have arrived right before the hold started. That meant they weren't opening her box anymore—not to deliver mail, and not to take out the outgoing mail. Another wave of dizziness hit me, and I had to lean against a tree and take a few deep breaths.

I didn't bother to mail my letter. I headed back to the cabin, trying to figure out why they would let me stay. Did they just trust me? I knew the answer to that. No. They wouldn't think it was okay to leave me in the mountains alone. Especially during winter. It had to be something else.

By the time I got back, my legs were tired, and I knew three things. #1: I had gotten what I wanted. I was staying. So, yay me. #2: My family was okay. #3: I better figure out what to do until Christmas.

I could wonder why my parents chose to leave me here later. For now, I needed to start my solo life in the Adirondacks. Just like Auntie Raven. But I'd do even better; I'd get my project done on top of it. I would *focus*. My parents would be impressed. Plus, I'd never have to hear Alex's stupid comments again. Auntie Raven would be proud of me, too. I couldn't lose.

Why didn't they tell Auntie Raven? my brain asked.

"Because Mama likes to hold a grudge," I answered.

Did they think she'd stay if they didn't show up?

I thought for a while, then said, "I don't know what any of these people are thinking. But I'll show them *all*."

I got an axe and started chopping more of the fallen tree in the clearing. I'd work on it a little each day until it was all added to the woodpile.

Each morning, I chopped until my arms ached, and every afternoon, I practiced my archery so I didn't get too bored . . . or lonely. My progress was slow, and October became November. I often worked in the rain, but I was surviving. I had been eating less and less, trying to make what I had last. My jeans were too loose, and I was exhausted, but every night, I worked on my project.

I thought about trying to reinforce the shed, but the idea was overwhelming. It would be a waste of energy, anyway. I knew what I really needed to do. I needed to get food. I needed to hunt.

November 6: Tomorrow, I'm going hunting. I don't want to. This is going to be the worst thing I've ever done in my life. I know it's what Auntie Raven would do.

The next day, I headed out as the sun came up. I packed my whistle, flashlight, knife, orange hat, extra socks, and gloves in my backpack. I slung the arrows over my shoulder and grabbed the bow. Her Majesty glared down at me, and Squarik and Squandré chattered. They sounded like they were cussing me out.

"What?" I yelled at them. "I don't have a choice, okay?" I watched my breath come out white and disappear into the cold air.

I hiked to the clearing and then beyond, where I'd seen the most rabbits. There was no way I could hit a bird.

I crouched down in the bushes and waited. My heart thudded in my ears, partly from the hike and partly from the panic I was struggling to keep from taking over me. It didn't take long for a rabbit to hop into view.

I had learned to be still because I liked to take pictures and draw the animals I saw on our hikes. If I moved or made noise, they ran away. I slowly raised my bow and aimed at the rabbit. It jerked its head in my direction and stared. Its little nose twitched. It hopped once and stopped. I waited to make sure it didn't move again. I didn't have the skill to hit a moving target.

I let the arrow fly. The arrow sailed about five feet to the right of the rabbit, and it darted away. Relief washed over me.

I knew I would have to hunt sooner or later, but for now, I'd have to figure out something else. I was starting to feel weak from not eating enough.

On my way back to the cabin, I looked for Squarik and Squandré, but they were gone. I yelled into the treetops. "I didn't do it. Are you happy?"

Inside the cabin, I started a fire and went to the kitchen. I stared into Auntie Raven's cabinets. It was time to get creative. I took down flour, salt, and sugar. I knew I needed more nutrition than that, so I took down cornmeal and peanut oil, too. I made up my own recipe and dumped the ingredients into a bowl. It was dry and chunky-looking, so I added water.

Eggs. Eggs would be the perfect addition. And I could probably get eggs without killing anything.

I'd hunt for nests tomorrow, but right now, I needed to eat something.

I made weird pancake patty things and cooked them in peanut oil. It smelled really good. I cooked the whole batch, so I'd have food stored. I nodded at myself and sat next to the fire with my plate.

I sniffed my golden patty and took a gigantic bite. It was disgusting. The patties were salty and grainy and flat and crunchy. If I had syrup, it wouldn't have helped. I ate it anyway, and threw the rest away.

Tomorrow, I would make more with less salt and more sugar. And if I found eggs, I could add one to the mix. Maybe at least then they would taste like nasty cookies.

I had been sleeping on the sofa every night. I liked watching the fire while I fell asleep, and I wanted to be close to the front door if my parents showed up. Tonight was different, though. I didn't check the windows one last time to see if car lights were approaching. I didn't think about how stupid they would feel when they saw me chillin' on the sofa next to a fire like the Queen of the Wilderness. Tonight, I stared into the fire. Tonight, I felt like I was forgetting something. I listened to the crackling and pulled a blanket around my shoulders.

They don't know Auntie Raven is gone.

That silent treatment Auntie Raven told you about wasn't a silent treatment.

Remember that email she sent? They never got it.

Because the email address was wrong.

And you knew it.

And you didn't say anything.

"Crap," I said.

14

I woke up exhausted and feeling guilty. My little attitude problem had created a big problem. My parents didn't know I was alone and neither did Auntie Raven. As far as my parents knew, I was busy with school. Plus, I had hoped to help Mama and Auntie Raven make up and act like actual sisters again. How was that going to happen now? I had ruined everything for everybody.

I could already hear the argument. Mama would blame Auntie Raven for not getting in touch again to confirm the plans. She'd be mad that Auntie Raven assumed she was giving her the silent treatment. Auntie Raven would be mad that Mama had acted in a way that would make her assume that in the first place. She'd feel like this was Mama blaming her, just like always. I had started a war.

And they'd *both* be mad at me. I was about to be on punishment for the rest of my life. I had one choice: Postpone the inevitable and survive my butt off so there was nothing they could blame each other for. It was the only way to make peace.

Rain pounded on the cabin roof. This was a much harder rain than any we'd had so far. I'd been trying to ignore what was happening in the Adirondacks: grayer skies and drizzles, early nightfall, dropping temperatures, and nights so cold I stayed inside. In the mornings, the garden was frosty.

This is the beginning of the end, I thought. *Winter is coming and I better get myself in gear today or die alone in the Adirondack Mountains.* I got the fire going and headed to the kitchen. Without thinking, I took my Nasty Patties out of the garbage. I was going to have to eat them. I took everything out of the cabinets to see if I could make anything else.

I found grits so old the white part of the box was yellow. The date stamped on the bottom was a year ago. Mama always threw expired food away, and Daddy always laughed at her and said those dates were really just suggestions to keep the company from getting sued. I cooked the grits, and when they were cool I formed patties to fry, which is what Daddy always did with leftover grits. Now I had Nasty Patties and grit cakes.

I put on Auntie Raven's too-big rain gear, packed the Mega Mountain backpack, grabbed the bow and arrows and the fishing pole, and set out. I wasn't coming back until I had enough food to wait out the storm.

I looked up as I walked, hoping to find a nest, and headed toward the stream where Auntie Raven had taught me to fish. I made it to the stream without finding a nest, so I cast my line and waited. I didn't want to waste all day fishing and getting nothing, and I was about to give up when I felt a little tug. I reeled in the line. At the end was a tiny fish. It was smaller than my hand, but it was protein, so I kept it. Before I left, I caught two more small fish. It wasn't exactly a feast, but I was proud of myself.

On my way back to the cabin, I noticed a nest in a nearby tree. It had been hidden on my way to the stream, but now I put my gear down and aimed an arrow at the nest. The rain falling on my face made it hard to see, and the first three times my arrows went wild. No birds flew away and that meant I wasn't in danger of killing a bird. I aimed again. This time, my arrow hit the nest and knocked it out of the tree into a pile of fallen leaves.

I don't know why I tiptoed up to it like it might attack me. I used an arrow to turn it right side up. Inside were three tiny eggs. I hadn't thought about how tiny the eggs would be, but I was accepting all donations today. The eggs hadn't even cracked, so I wrapped them in one of my extra socks.

Then a horrible thought hit me. *What if there are baby birds in the eggs?* I was losing my mind or something. Why did I assume I'd find some grocery store eggs in a nest in the wilderness?

My stomach rose to my chest as I unwrapped the eggs. If there were birds in them, maybe I could put them back. Would the fall have killed them? But if there were no birds inside, I would be wasting good food.

In one egg, I made a crack small enough to keep in an edible egg. It was impossible to see inside, though. I took a deep breath and made a bigger crack. I peeled off a piece of shell.

"Oh no!" I yelled.

I cradled the egg in my hands. "I'm sorry, little baby bird."

A wave of nausea doubled me over and I threw up all over the ground. I backed away from it and sat there for what felt like an hour. Then I picked up the nest, put all three eggs back in it, and climbed as high as I could in the tree. I put the nest in a branch.

"I'm so sorry," I whispered before I climbed back down. I had probably just murdered three baby birds for no reason at all. This was the last time. No more hunting.

I gathered my arrows and left. This was the worst thing I'd ever done in my life. All I had to show for a whole day of foraging were three tiny fish that I was now too queasy to eat.

At least I had the food I'd cooked. I could eat that and have a tiny bit of fish if I got desperate. It was enough to live on for at least a few days.

Halfway home, fresh pawprints crossed the muddy path and I stopped to look at them. They were definitely coyote prints, and from what I could tell, there were two or three. I picked up my pace. I should have never left the cabin. For the rest of the storm, I would stay in and do my homework.

Mama always checked the weather forecast because she was always thinking about hair. My hair, her hair, clients' hair. She would know there was a huge storm in the mountains. I wondered if she'd think about me.

I realized I hadn't conditioned my braids since Auntie Raven left. I'd have to do that tonight. Mama had worked hard to help me grow my hair back after I convinced her to let me get it straightened for Christmas two years ago and it broke off. I could practically hear her now: *Ava! WHAT HAPPENED TO YOUR HAIR? Didn't you use the conditioner I sent?*

I laughed and scared a squirrel out of the bushes. It startled me out of my daydream and back into reality. I needed to be able to eat if I was going to survive the winter. To distract myself, I counted my footsteps all the way back to the cabin.

On my way to put the fish in the refrigerator, I

stepped in a wet spot on the floor. I kneeled down to see what it was, and something dripped on my head. The roof was leaking. It wasn't a big leak, but it was steady. When Auntie Raven and I were fixing the fence, she had said the cabin needed work, too. This must have been what she meant. I ran out to the garden for a bucket and set it under the drip.

I did my best to stay positive and work on my project. I was determined to stay on schedule so I had time to get ready for winter. I was glad I had mailed everything due before Thanksgiving already, but I didn't have a way to mail the project when it was due. Maybe if I mailed it in by winter break, my teacher would understand. Maybe they'd also excuse whatever assignments I missed in December—the ones I didn't even know about because I couldn't go to the library and check emails.

The wind kicked up while I was eating dinner, and the power went out. I turned on the lanterns and placed one on the table and one in the bathroom. I put another log on the fire and made a bed next to it. I tried to pretend I was sitting by a campfire instead of alone in a cabin with no power during a storm.

Every once in a while, there was a huge gust of wind and a whistling sound. The rain pounded on the roof and the sides of the cabin. Debris hit the windows. The Big Bad Wolf had arrived and was trying to blow the house in.

But I wasn't giving up. *Not today, Wolf. Not by the hair on my chinny chin chin.*

15

A creaking sound woke me up in the middle of the night. At first, I thought I had been dreaming about being back at home. The floor upstairs always creaked when our neighbors walked around, especially if they were vacuuming or had company. But it wasn't a dream.

The sound was coming from outside—somewhere close. I swiveled my head like an owl. The creak was coming from Auntie Raven's garden, loud enough to hear over the rain and wind. Auntie Raven and I had just fixed the garden fence. Could it be loose and creaking already? Maybe, but not *this* loud. I closed my eyes and ignored my pounding heart.

BOOM.

Thunder rumbled through the Adirondacks and

the whole cabin shook. I jumped up from my make-shift bed next to the dwindling fire and stood still. Waiting.

BOOM.

Creak.

Her Majesty. The creaking was my beautiful pine tree. I ran a few steps toward the window to look, then realized how stupid that was. If the storm broke the window, the glass would hit me in the face, so I ran back to my mound of blankets. Even though I had only taken about seven steps, I was panting.

Creak.

BOOM! CRACK!

It sounded like the earth itself was splitting open. A light strobed outside, lighting the cabin even through the thick curtains. Lightning. If any-one had told me I would be afraid of a storm one day, I would have laughed in their face. Storms were just a part of nature.

Unless you were in the Adirondack Mountains. By yourself.

Another bolt of lightning flashed, and then a cracking-creaking-crackling-crashing sound followed it. I ran to the corner, squatted, and covered my ears with my hands. My legs were shaking so much, I thought I might topple over.

My mind raced until it settled on the safety drills at school. Stop, drop, and roll for fire. Duck and cover for earthquakes or explosions.

Duck and cover.

I kneeled and curled over my legs, then clasped my hands over the back of my neck. I wasn't under anything, like a desk, but it was better than nothing. The wooden floor was hard against my knees. I squeezed my eyes shut. Colors swirled on the backs of my eyelids. I hoped I wasn't about to faint.

The wind howled and the sound of wood splintering rose above the storm with a whoosh and then a deafening crash. I screamed into my legs. Something rained down on me, but it wasn't water. A gust of wind forced its way through the cabin, bringing with it the smell of the forest and the chill of the night.

I stayed in the duck-and-cover position—frozen in the corner. There would be no announcement that this was only a drill. No bell would ring to tell me the drill was over. I struggled to breathe through my scrunched-up chest and wondered how long I should stay like this. And what I would see when I got up.

I opened one eye. The wind had blown out the fire. I opened the other eye and gasped.

Her Majesty was a looming shadow inside the cabin. Her branches stretched toward me like dark arms with pointed fingers. The smell of pine and smoke filled my nostrils. If I was outside having a campfire with Auntie Raven, I would have loved the smell. But right now, it was the smell of disaster.

Everything was ruined. The cabin. My food. My plans. My future. The home of all Her Majesty's royal subjects—my friends. *Me*. Her Majesty was the strongest, most beautiful tree I'd ever seen. She wasn't supposed to fall.

"No!" I yelled. "No, no, no, no, no!"

I hugged myself. The roof could cave in all the way and break every bone in my body. Nobody would even know. I'd be laying on the cabin floor decaying. Coyotes and wolves and foxes would eat me. I didn't want to die. My entire body trembled, until one big shiver shook me into action.

The cabin wasn't safe. I had to get outside. The door was only about ten feet from my corner. I didn't want to accidentally cause the tree to fall more or make the cabin shift and crumble, so I got down on all fours and crawled toward the door.

I lifted my hand to turn the doorknob, and a coyote in the distance howled. A second coyote howled in response, and this one sounded like it was on the porch. Maybe the close one was a lost baby coyote . . . or maybe they were hunting. I couldn't go out there. Outside was just as dangerous. I didn't have any shelter, and it was cold and wet—I could catch pneumonia and die. I had no flashlight or warm clothes and even if I took my blankets, they would be soaked in minutes. Plus, something worse than a coyote, like a bear, might attack me.

Panic sent another shiver through me. I inhaled for four counts and exhaled for four counts, like Carlos did sometimes. It took me five breaths before I could think straight.

Because of the way Her Majesty fell, the roof

was caving in toward the middle of the cabin. That meant the walls parallel to the tree trunk were the safest. If the roof caved all the way in, those walls would be the most likely to stay up. I had to stay inside.

I crawled toward the corner again, feeling for Auntie Raven's rocking chair. My hand found the bottom of the chair, and it rocked forward and slammed into my forehead. If I lived through the night, I was going to have a big knot on my head. And a headache. Before the rocking chair could rebound and come back to hit me again, I stopped it and pulled it to the wall, next to the corner.

With my back against the wall, I tipped the rocking chair forward until the headrest leaned against the wall above my head. It formed a little triangle that protected the entire front of my body. My back was protected by the wall. I shivered.

The cabin was getting colder by the minute with the roof open. Moisture and cold air filled the room. It was almost as bad as being outside. The rain wasn't reaching me, but I still needed to get my blankets and pillow. I didn't want to leave my little rocking chair shelter, though. The roof might cave in while I was getting my covers. But the shelter wouldn't help me if I froze to death.

I crawled as fast as I could until my hand touched the blankets. I grabbed them and draped them over my back. I clutched my pillow in one hand and Pokey in the other and turned to crawl back. I could feel the bruises forming on my knees.

Thunder rolled through the mountains again, and Her Majesty creaked and shifted. A branch broke off and fell on my leg. It felt like I had been stabbed in the calf. I winced, which made my forehead pound. I ignored my knees and fast-crawled toward the corner.

I got back into my position against the wall. My calf throbbed against the floor. I padded it with a blanket and then wrapped the rest of the blanket over the top of my legs. Then I folded a blanket to put over my head and back. I used the last two as cover for my body. I pulled the chair forward and tilted it against the wall and shoved the pillow between the chair and my chest. I tucked Pokey under the pillow, near my heart. Finally, I hooked my feet around the rung under the chair to keep it from slipping. My only goal now was to make it through the night.

Outside, the storm roared and the coyote near the cabin howled again.

Inside, I buried my face in my pillow and sobbed.

16

At some point, I realized it was dawn, because the cabin was getting brighter. The light was coming in through the gaping hole in the ceiling. Her Majesty looked like a fallen soldier, and seeing her sideways was an unwelcome reminder that even the grandest of us can suddenly come crashing down.

From my rocking chair cage, I watched the sun come up as if it had never rained at all. My head throbbed and the wound on my calf ached to the rhythm of my heartbeat. I wondered what happened to Squarik and Squandré, and the beetles and birds, and the army of ants, and whatever other small creatures called Her Majesty home. We were all homeless now. Obviously, my stay in the little cabin in the woods was over.

My feelings toward morning were mixed. I was glad not to be in the dark, but I also knew morning brought with it some serious decisions. The first thing I had to do was leave my cage.

I slowly set the rocking chair right and pushed it back with my feet so I could unfold myself. My body was stiff, and I was scared to move. Scared to look at my leg. Scared that standing would upset the status quo and send the entire roof down on my swollen head.

Instead of getting up, I made mental notes of the cabin. Her Majesty had cut the cabin into two halves: the front and the back. This half of the house was shaped sort of like a backward lean-to. The tree had taken out the kitchen, so I couldn't get to my food or anything else there. The bedroom was blocked, too. The table and everything on it were soaked. My textbooks were ruined. My map and unfinished charting project were worthless. I'd be getting zero points. Not only was I going to be the kid who couldn't get her report card because they had a textbook debt, but I was also the kid who didn't want their report card anyway, because it was all Fs. On top of that, nothing normal was left—nothing to distract me from my messed up situation.

Everything against my wall was still dry—the blankets and pillows, my journal near the fireplace, my backpack, and the Mega Mountain backpack by the door. The bow and arrows were laying on the floor where I left them, too.

I stood up and limped backward toward the wall. Before I gathered anything, I needed to check my body. I pulled off my sweatpants and looked at my knees. They were bruised but they'd be okay. Next, I checked my calf. There was a big gash across it. Blood had dripped down and soaked my sock, but I would have to wear it for now. If I were at home, Mama would clean my leg and probably take me to the doctor. I didn't think I needed stitches, but my leg needed to be cleaned and bandaged . . . with water and bandages I didn't have.

I put my pants back on and took off my sweatshirt. My upper body was fine, except for what looked like a splinter in the crease of my arm, right where my elbow made my arm bend. I didn't know how I would have gotten a splinter there. I squinted at it and tried to rub it off. But it wasn't a splinter. It was a tick.

Panic returned as all the tick facts I had learned raced through my mind. They bore themselves into your skin and could cause infections. They needed to be removed as soon as possible. You weren't supposed to squeeze them or pull them out with your fingernails, because they might leave their heads stuck inside you. You also weren't supposed to burn them out or pour stuff on them. If they were deer ticks and stayed in too long, they could give you Lyme disease. And if Lyme disease went untreated . . .

The worst part of this was that it was my fault. Just like everything else. I had completely forgotten to put on bug spray yesterday. I always sprayed my whole body and my shoes, and I tucked my pants into my socks and sprayed them before I left the cabin. If I died of Lyme disease, it was my own stupid fault.

I put my sweatshirt back on. There was nothing I could do about the Tick That Might Kill Me right now. I had to get out of here with as many helpful materials as possible. I put on my shoes and got to work.

I opened the door slowly and waited to see if the cabin would fall. It didn't. I took out the most important things first. The bow and arrows, the fishing pole, the backpacks, and the rain gear sat safely beyond the porch. Next, I took out the blankets and pillows, Pokey, and my journal. I remembered there were matches and a lighter on the mantle, so I went back for those. Then I got a brilliant idea and went back three more times to get the sofa cushions. When I was done, I softly shut the door, hoping it might hold up the rest of the house.

I stood with my pile of supplies and stared at the house. Her Majesty's branches reached for the sky from the middle of the roof. The side of the house that bore the weight of her trunk sagged. Auntie Raven would be devastated. I wondered if she would fix it or move away. Apparently, I would *not* be moving away. I would be suffering the consequences of my dinner table demand to go live out in nature.

"Are you happy now, Ava?" I asked myself. Then I plopped down on a sofa cushion with no sofa and cried. I had no place to live, and it was my fault. Nobody was coming to help me, and that was my fault, too. I didn't even have any food. Plus, I was flunking sixth grade, and I had formed a mountain between my mama and my auntie that neither of them would be willing to climb. Auntie Raven's words came back to me: *Nature has a way of knocking you to your knees.*

I started cackling. I had literally been knocked to my knees. Then the fact that I was laughing made me wonder if insanity was an early sign of Lyme disease and I stopped.

It reminded me of what Alex used to say when we played Go Fish. If he asked for a card I didn't have and had to go fish and then got what he asked for, he said, *Fished my wish* in an annoying voice. I had fished my wish, but it didn't look like I was winning this game.

With my first decisions made, and the results scattered all over the yard, I decided to inspect the house. I walked around to see how bad it was. The garden was partly covered by Her Majesty, but not all of it. Later, I'd go see if I could find anything to eat. On the other side of the house, the top of Her Majesty had landed on a cluster of treetops. I wondered how long they would hold her up. I walked all the way around her, instead of ducking under. The back of the house was like the front. The wall still stood. I was too scared to get close enough to peek through the window, so I continued to the far side of the house.

From here, I could see the other side of Her Majesty, but that wasn't the worst part of this view. There was also a dead squirrel. I recognized him right away.

17

I ran to Squarik and kneeled next to him. There were no wounds, so I guessed he died from impact. Or maybe he had a heart attack. I stroked his fur for the first time. My poor little friend. Tears rained down on his lifeless body.

Furious with the Adirondacks for betraying me, I marched to the edge of the garden, got Auntie Raven's little garden shovel, and dug a hole at the base of where Her Majesty used to stand. I buried Squarik there, and then put a ring of pine cones around his grave. Where was Squandré? For the first time, it occurred to me that maybe they were mates. Either way, Squandré was probably even more devasted than me.

They didn't deserve this. Dizzy with exhaustion

and grief, I closed my eyes and felt myself falling asleep.

I woke up with my stomach growling when the sun was high in the sky. I also needed to pee. When I stood up, everything around me spun, and I had to wait a few minutes before I walked back to my pile of belongings. Nowhere in that pile was there toilet paper. I roamed into the woods a few steps and did what I needed to do. When I finished, I wiggled to try to shake off the drips, which didn't work. Tomorrow, I'd need to find something to wipe with. For now, I had other things to do. Especially if I was going to keep myself alive.

Part of me wanted to go to town for cinnamon rolls and toilet paper. Another part of me wanted to go to the library and ask if I could call home, but I was positive I couldn't make it all the way there on foot. My legs were wobbly just walking back from the mailbox, and that was when I still had food in the fridge. Town was way farther than that. I didn't trust myself to find my way to town anyway. Besides, what could I possibly say to Mama that wouldn't make things worse?

I got myself into this situation, and I was going to have to get myself out.

Whether I found food or not, I knew the first thing I needed was a fire. I cleaned up Auntie's fire pit and was grateful to find her stash of wood still covered with the tarp.

Once the fire was going, I went to the garden to see if there was anything I could eat. I found a small pumpkin but decided to look for something else before I cut it from the vine. There were a few scraggly looking cucumbers hanging from a plant in the corner, so I cut one off. Then I remembered Auntie Raven had planted seed potatoes. I wasn't sure what potato plants looked like, but I did know the potatoes themselves grew under the ground. Something leafy was growing against the fence not far from where we had buried the potato pieces, but there was nothing that looked edible growing on it. I got down on my sore knees and started pulling them up.

I hit the potato jackpot. I found three right away. Since I couldn't eat three, I stopped digging. At least I knew where to find food now. It didn't solve the protein problem, but it would get me through today.

After I rubbed two potatoes clean with my jeans, I cut them up and put them in my little mess kit pot. I headed to the garden to get water, and realized Her Majesty was blocking the faucet. For all I knew, the pipe was broken anyway. I would just have to eat dry, unseasoned potatoes, which turned out to be delicious since I was delirious and starving. I rinsed my potatoes down with the cucumber.

Next, I needed shelter. Even though there were no clouds in the sky, I wanted something that would last. There was no way I was sleeping on the porch. It was too close to the house. I eyed the shed. I already knew it was dangerous, so sleeping inside was out of the question. The few times Auntie Raven needed something out of it, she wouldn't even let me go in. But Auntie Raven wasn't here. I was. And inside that shed was the tent.

A padlock hung on the door, but it wasn't latched. I pulled it off, opened the door, and glanced around. There were storage bins and things that looked old and broken all over the place. I was relieved to see the tent just inside. Without stepping all the way in, I grabbed it. I pitched the tent on the side of the house near the fire pit. It was close enough for me to see if someone came, but far enough away to be safe if the cabin caved all the way in. I put the sofa cushions in a line down the middle of the tent, then made my bed on top of them. I stored all my equipment on one side and set up an emergency pile on the other—a flashlight, knife, matches, lighter, bug spray . . . and whistle.

As the sun set, I dragged the two chairs off the porch, just in case I needed them for something. I sat on one and put my feet on the other. I drew the destroyed house in my journal and remembered Alex's words at the dinner table: "I hope this doesn't turn into one of those survival stories." Under my picture I wrote, *November 9: I had no idea how right I was when I told Alex I would be learning all the survival skills. It won't be Alex I have to show, though. It'll be myself, because I'm not sure I can do this.*

I crawled into my tent, zipped the opening shut,

and laid down. My leg reminded me it still needed to be cleaned and wrapped. My head begged for a pain killer. My heart hurt most of all, though.

I had managed to mess up everything I loved, and now I had to fix it by staying alive.

18

The next morning, I got dizzy when I tried to sit up, so I laid back down. Had the rocking chair given me a concussion? My head pounded and my calf throbbed. They were like twins competing for attention. I didn't feel like getting up anyway, so I laid on my back while tears rolled into my ears. The wilderness had turned on me.

I thought about Carlos playing video games and Sienna reading and doing whatever it was she did on her videos. I thought about Kimberly's version of "camp," and it suddenly didn't sound as bad. Finally, my growling stomach forced me up.

I sat up slowly and waited for the dizziness to pass. Once my vision cleared, I checked the tick in my arm. So far, the skin wasn't puffy or red or itchy.

It just looked like a bug that might be carrying a deadly disease was stuck in my skin. My leg had started to scab over, and it was sticking to my pants, so as soon as I pulled them down, the wound started bleeding again. It was never going to heal that way. I had to force myself to get it together.

I used my new bathroom behind the tree, and ate a potato and a cucumber for breakfast. I made myself find something positive to think about. It took a long time, but eventually I thanked nature for another day of no rain. As much as I wanted to go back to sleep, I didn't let myself. I had to stay alive. I grabbed the fishing pole, backpack, and the pot from my mess kit. From now on, I would fish every day. It would give me something to do, so I wouldn't start losing it like people in the movies.

My boots felt like they were made out of iron, but I trudged along anyway. Almost immediately, something tugged on my line. It was bigger than the tiny fish I caught last time, and I had to stand up to reel it in. But as soon as I got to my feet, I stepped wrong on the muddy bank of the stream and fell into the cold water. Because I was trying not to lose my fish, I didn't break the fall with my hands and landed face-first. I used my fury to push myself up onto my knees and reel in the fish. It was bigger than my hand, and I was pretty sure it was some kind of trout. I wished I could catch more, but I didn't have any way to store it and keep it fresh. One would have to do.

I waded out of the water into the cold air. It felt like tiny pins were pricking my skin, and I knew right away my clothes weren't going to dry any time soon. Hopefully, the water wasn't full of bacteria that would get into the cut on my leg. I filled my pot with water and headed back, stiff and squelching all the way.

At my camp, I started a fire and sat as close as I could while I filleted my fish. I put my fish and my pot of water on the fire. I would drink part of the water and use the rest to rinse my leg. In the meantime, I would sit under the sun in my chairs with my feet up and try to dry off. I drew a picture of my fish and wrote, *November 10: Catch of the Day: trout*. Then I turned the page and wrote something that had been on my mind for at least a week. Something I didn't want to think about.

My birthday is coming. On November 19th, I'll be twelve. I won't have a party or a cake or presents or friends or family. I'll probably still be sitting in this stupid chair, wet and cold.

Like I had conjured it, a cold breeze blew and raised goose bumps on my skin. I wished the goose bumps could push out the tick. The air got even colder after I ate, forcing me into the tent, where I did something I would have never imagined I would do. And something I would never tell anyone about.

I stripped off all my clothes. Underwear, too. I used a blanket to dry off my damp skin, then turned it around and wrapped myself in the dry side. I remembered my extra socks and put them on. I stood there cackling like a weirdo. I was naked with socks on, wrapped in a blanket, like some kind of wild mountain person. I smelled like a wild person, too. I couldn't remember when I last bathed, and the stream didn't leave me smelling any fresher. I was warmer, though, and that was what mattered.

I left the tent like that, and with one arm and shoulder exposed, I fed the fire, put the chairs next to it, and hung my wet clothes over them. I put my boots right next to the fire pit. Then I rinsed my leg. Once the blood and dirt were rinsed off, I could see that the wound wasn't as bad as I thought. It seemed to be healing. I left my leg sticking out of the blanket for as long as I could stand it, so it would dry and form a scab.

The temperature dropped way down that night, so I went to the tent early, and soon enough, coyotes started howling. I hadn't heard coyotes during my nights with Auntie Raven and wondered why they were so noisy now. The yips and howls got closer, and I zipped up my tent. I sat on my bed with my whistle.

I must have fallen asleep sitting up because that's how I was when a rustling sound woke me up. It sounded a lot like the animal I heard when Auntie Raven took me camping. Only this time, it didn't go away. I heard it knock something over outside and realized that my leftover fish was still near the fire. I completely forgot to put it in the bear-resistant canister. Whatever it was must have been eating my leftovers and knocked over the pot. If I survived tonight, I would have to be more careful about what I left out. It was like all the local wildlife got a message that there was fresh meat out here. And the fresh meat was me.

After a while, the creature rustled closer to the tent—so close it brushed against the outside. I gasped and sat as still as possible. There was more rustling that sounded like it was a few feet away. I didn't know what was out there, but there were two of them.

There was a sniffing sound and then something *pawed* at the side of the tent. I jumped up to grab my knife and whistle, and my blanket dropped. I knew I wasn't supposed to, but I said a bad word. I wrapped up again and closed my eyes so I could concentrate on what I heard. I kept my breathing even and quiet, despite my thudding heart.

It pawed again and the zipper jingled. Then there was a snarl and the scuffling sound of two animals fighting. They bumped the tent hard enough to shake it. I wanted to stab them but didn't want to cut a slit in my tent. The fighting and snarling continued.

I blew into my whistle, but the little ball inside

stuck. The whistle made a pitiful, half-hearted sound, but there was a pause in the fighting. I blew it again, hard enough to make sure the animals knew I meant business, and it worked. They scampered away.

I sat on the cushions and pulled the blankets tighter. I focused on my breathing to slow my heart rate down. The last thing I needed was to faint or something and be found naked in a tent with a whistle and a knife in my hands.

I didn't even try to sleep. In fact, I did the opposite. I needed a new plan. I couldn't do this every night. At the very least, I needed to wear clothes in case I had to get away fast.

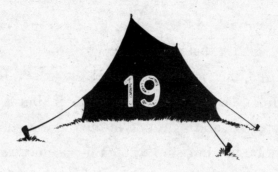

I hit the sides of my tent and made a bunch of noise before I came out the next morning, just in case anything was still lurking around out there. I unzipped a corner of the tent and peeked out. The dirt was full of tracks and signs of a struggle. But the tracks leading away from my camp were tiny. *Raccoons.*

I looked at the fire pit and saw I was right—the raccoons ate my fish. My clothes were still wet, so I was stuck wearing the blanket. I wasn't going to get anything done like this. I walked to the back side of the house and examined it. It looked exactly the same as it did last time I checked it. I inched closer and peeked through the bedroom window. My suitcases sat against the wall, right where I left them. It was hard to believe I had been miserable living out of suitcases while I waited for my parents to come. I'd kill to have that problem now.

I eyed the dresser. I had never gone through Auntie Raven's drawers or her closet, but now I wondered what I might find in there. I was going to have to bump things up a notch if I planned to survive out here. Sitting around naked in a tent feeling sorry for myself until Christmas wasn't going to cut it.

I picked up a big rock, hurled it at the window, and ran away as the glass shattered. I wasn't worried about the glass, but if the house caved in, I didn't want to be under it like I was in some kind of *Wizard of Oz* remix. I waited long enough to make sure the house wasn't going to collapse. The rock had made a hole, but I was too big to fit through it. Plus, I didn't want to cut myself climbing in.

I threw a bigger rock, which thudded against the side of the house and fell to the ground. So instead of another rock, I found a big stick, broke the rest of the glass with it, and smoothed the edges so I could climb through.

I was so weak, I couldn't even hoist up my own weight, especially while I was wrapped in a blanket. I got a chair and tried to climb through the window. My leg kept getting tangled in the blanket, so I did what I had to do. I glanced around to make sure I was alone, laid the blanket over the jagged window-sill, and climbed through the window naked, avoiding the glass on the floor when I landed.

As fast as I could, I rummaged through the draw-ers and closet. I threw anything that looked halfway useful out the window. I was glad Auntie Raven hated technology, because if she had any hidden cameras, I'd have to destroy this evidence. I didn't take the time to judge the items. If I might need it, out the window it went. An umbrella, three pairs of shoes, my smallest suitcase, and all the contents of the one too big to lift through the window.

I caught sight of myself in the mirror and it wasn't pretty. My braids were a mess, I had a lumpy bruise on my forehead, and I looked way too thin. I promised myself I'd try to find a way to eat more. Next, I rifled through the nightstand. I chucked Tylenol, lip balm, a head scarf, and the blankets from the bed out the window. Then I tossed out an empty laundry basket. I guess the adrenaline was pumping, because I pulled myself up on the window-sill with no problem and jumped down. I fell and rolled a couple of times.

It was quite a haul. I stood in the middle of it and got dressed in two layers: leggings and jeans, a hoodie and a coat. Then, with my pants falling down, I started moving it all to my camp. In the pile of clothes I had never worn, I found a candy bar and a bag of chips I hadn't brought. There was a sticky note on it from Alex. It said, "Just in case."

"Alex," I said out loud. "In case is here."

For once, Alex's little smart comment didn't bother me. In fact, Alex had cheered me up. I smiled and decided to save the treats for my birthday. I put them just inside the shed and hung the lock through the hole. The raccoons were *not* getting my birthday dinner.

The most important things went inside the tent, and I packed the rest in my suitcase. I hid it under the tarp with the woodpile.

Feeling satisfied with myself, I went to the

garden and dug up three more potatoes and cut off another cucumber. I ate the cucumber right away, then cooked all three of the potatoes. For some reason, I could only finish about half of my food, so I left the rest in the pot and kept it warm for later.

There was nothing else I had to do, so I added wood to the fire and sat on the ground next to it. I tried to remember what day of the week it was, but I only knew the date. Was it a school day? I hadn't been the same since the rocking chair hit my head. I couldn't remember how many days ago that was, either.

"I need to get some sleep," I said to the fire. I laid down in the warmth and dozed off.

A deafening crash woke me up. The fire was out but still warm. Something was falling on me. It was either dawn or dusk, and leaves and pine needles were on my arms. When I sat up, more fell out of my hair. I looked around.

Her Majesty had come loose from the treetops that held her up and she had fallen all the way down. The house was now completely split in half, and the walls that had been left standing straight were now crooked.

"I could have been killed," I said. "I could have been in there when this happened. They would have found me inside dead and naked with a bunch of stuff thrown out the window. They would have thought I'd lost my mind."

I started to cry. I didn't know why I was crying—maybe because I was safe and had gotten everything I needed before the cabin crumbled; maybe because I could have been too close when the tree fell and been hurt. There was one thing I knew for sure. I needed to stop all this crying.

My mind was foggy. I was scared I was losing track of time, so I grabbed my journal and wrote, *November 11 (maybe): tree crashed*. My handwriting didn't look right and I was shaky. I took a bunch of Carlos breaths, but they made me feel like I was hyperventilating. I felt like people on TV look when they're having a heart attack. Did almost-twelve-year-olds have heart attacks?

I ate my leftover potatoes and watched the sky to see if the sun was going up or down. It was setting.

Relieved I hadn't lost a whole day, I crawled into the tent. I zipped it up and laid on my back. I was thirsty. *Extremely* thirsty.

I stared up into the darkening sky. The stars were just starting to appear. Part of my brain told me something was wrong with that.

20

I was in and out of weird dreams all night long. In one dream, I was a raccoon under a blanket. In another, Squarik was handing me seeds and I was planting them in the garden. In a third, I was having a birthday party, but it looked like the Mad Hatter's Tea Party.

Each time, I woke up disoriented and focused on the stars until I fell asleep again. Something wet was dripping on my face when I woke up. There were no stars, and I remembered there weren't supposed to be any. I was inside the tent. Maybe I had been hallucinating. And what was falling on my face?

I turned on my flashlight and aimed it at the top of the tent. It was ripped open and it was raining outside. Had the raccoons ripped it? I staggered outside with the flashlight and found a branch laying against the back side of my tent. Maybe when Her Majesty crashed through the treetops, a branch flew over here and punctured the tent on its way down.

I growled. This was not good. The hole was too big to ignore or repair. There was something else I finally had to admit, too. I couldn't keep living in this tent. It wasn't made for winter. For now, I would have to take the tarp off the wood pile and cover my tent with it. My wood would be wet, but it was better than having my bed soaked or having an uninvited guest drop in in the middle of the night.

I dragged my suitcase into my tent, secured the tarp with rocks, set my damp blanket aside, and collapsed onto the bed. Within seconds, I fell asleep again.

When I woke up again, it was morning. The sky was gray, but the rain had stopped, and it was so cold it made the bridge of my nose hurt. I went to get wood for a fire, but when I tried to light the kindling, all I got was smoke. It was too wet.

I threw one piece of firewood after another off the pile, trying to get to the bottom. I prayed that it was dry under there. Eventually, I did find several dry pieces of wood, but they were much too big to be kindling. I considered burning some clothes, but that seemed like a bad idea. If I was here until Christmas, I would need those clothes. I'd probably have to wear them all at the same time to stay warm.

Everything around me was wet—the pine cones and pine needles, the sticks on the ground. There was no way I was going back in the house to find something, and even if I did, I was absolutely *not* burning books.

My body ached and shook. I was going to have to do something. I got my knife. I let out a wild scream and sawed off several of my braids. Through my tears, I stared at the severed hair in my hand.

Mama had spent hundreds of Sundays on my hair. Washing. Deep conditioning. Oiling my scalp. I sat on a stool and she sat behind me to style it while I watched cartoons. She even took special requests—twists, braids, Afro puffs, side parts, and baby hairs. Then she wrapped my head like a gift.

I got tired of sitting there sometimes and complained. I winced and whined if she pulled it too tight. Never realizing, until right now, that she did it because she loved me. And I was throwing it into the fire.

"I'm sorry, Mama," I said. "I love you, too."

This better work, I thought. Using my braids as kindling, I built a fire. It did work. Once it got nice and big, I crept as close as I dared to the cabin window. I barely recognized my reflection. I looked malnourished and now I had braids hanging down one side of my face, and braid stubs sticking out on the other side. I turned away from myself and put on more layers of clothes. Crying the whole time, I drank the rainwater that had fallen into my pot.

Then I ate my candy bar. Saving it was stupid. I was starving and weak. I might be dead by my birthday anyway. I took itty-bitty bites and chewed as many times as I could. It had peanuts and caramel wrapped in chocolate and it was the most delicious thing I had ever eaten. It definitely beat the heck out of potatoes and cucumbers.

The water and candy had perked me up quite

a bit, and I felt better. Better enough to know I was going to have to do what I said I'd never do. I was going to have to kill something.

I packed the small backpack with the necessities and slung my arrows over my shoulder. I sprayed my whole body with bug spray twice. Then I stood there second-guessing my decision until I remembered my reflection.

"Ava, you don't have a choice," I said.

"I know I don't," I said back.

And then I walked away from my camp without looking back.

21

I knew exactly where I was going and what I was looking for. I wanted a rabbit. I knew it was too much food, but it was a big enough target, and I needed protein if I was going to survive. Somewhere, I had heard that rabbit tasted like chicken, and chicken sounded delicious right now.

I hunched down in the bushes like I had done before, but one thing was different. This time, I was serious. This time, I wouldn't hesitate, and I wasn't going home empty-handed.

Within minutes a nice, plump rabbit hopped into view. I slowly raised my arrow and took aim. The arrow flew toward the rabbit, but it was about an inch off, so it sailed past the animal and landed in the brush. The rabbit ran away.

While I waited for another one, I took a few practice shots, and they were dead-on. I would get the next one. "Little Peter Cottontail doesn't have a chance," I said. Then I felt both giddy and guilty at the same time.

The next rabbit was a baby bunny. I aimed at it but couldn't do it. I was hungry, maybe even starving, but there was no way I was killing another baby animal. But before I had time to put my bow down, a bigger rabbit hopped into view—the mama. I aimed at her, but before I could shoot my arrow, I burst into tears.

Not only was I incapable of killing the mama and leaving the baby an orphan, I was jealous of the baby for having a mother. I missed my own Mama. I missed her doing my hair. I missed her spaghetti and meatballs. I missed her blasting music and singing off-key in the car.

I was a whole entire mess. Even when I was on the verge of starvation, I didn't have what it took to survive. Alex was right.

What happened next caught me completely off guard. A coyote tore out of the bushes and grabbed the baby rabbit in its mouth. Without thinking, I shot an arrow at the coyote and hit it in the chest. My arrow sunk in deep, and the coyote yowled and then fell, silent. The mama rabbit took off, and the baby fell out of the coyote's mouth. Neither animal moved.

I waited for a while to see what would happen. Would the baby hop away and find its mama? Was there another coyote nearby waiting to pounce? I wondered if this was one of the coyotes I'd been hearing. When the forest stayed quiet, I crept over to the two injured animals.

The coyote was still breathing, but it didn't move. I poked it with an arrow, but it didn't respond. The bunny was dead. It had puncture wounds in its neck from the coyote, and it looked like its neck was broken.

I didn't want to leave an arrow in the coyote, because I might need it later, but I was scared to pull it out. I picked up the bunny by its ears, so I wouldn't get blood on my hands, and heard a faint snapping sound as a bone in its little neck broke. The coyote didn't seem to be breathing and didn't follow me with its eyes. I was almost positive it was dead.

I removed my arrow and backed away. In that moment, I realized how completely ridiculous this whole situation was. I couldn't kill the baby rabbit or its mama, but I killed a coyote trying to protect them. Now I was going to cook the baby and eat it for dinner. If I didn't eat it, some other creature would. That's how nature worked. And now I was more a part of nature than I was a girl from Manhattan. I was officially part of the Adirondack food chain.

Before I went back to my camp, I gathered my arrows and got water from the stream. I was determined to eat and drink enough to stay alert. All the way home, I thought about how to skin a rabbit. I had no idea what I was doing. I wondered if cutting the rabbit would be a bloody process. I had been surprised by how little blood a fish had. Were rabbits different? What part of the rabbit were you supposed to eat? It suddenly sounded disgusting, and I wasn't sure if I could go through with it.

Some of the smaller pieces of wood had dried while I was gone, and I built a fire without using any more of my braids. While my water boiled, I stared at the bunny on the ground.

"If you're gonna do it, do it," I told myself.

I decided to approach it like the filleting of a fish. I made a cut straight down the middle from the back of the rabbit's neck to its tail. It was bloody, but it didn't gush all over the place. Then I made cuts going around its body and got the fur and skin off by putting my knife underneath and separating it from the meat. After I got the skin off, I ran to the bushes and threw up.

Nothing was going to make me waste this food, though, so I continued cutting until I had little chunks of meat. The pieces were the size of the meat in Mama's stew, which gave me an idea. I drank some of the water, then put the rabbit meat in the pot. I got a potato and cut it up and added it to the pot, too. I scoured the garden to see if there was anything at all that might give the food some flavor. There was some kind of herb still growing in the herb garden. I sniffed it. It was either rosemary or thyme, and I couldn't remember which. I didn't care anyway. I threw some of that in the pot, too.

I wished I knew how to use all the rabbit, but I didn't have a clue and I felt guilty for wasting it. While my dinner cooked, I dug a small hole far away from my camp and buried the parts of the rabbit I didn't use. The last thing I needed was raccoons and coyotes fighting over my leftovers in the middle of the night. Then I cleaned the bloody arrow by rubbing it on damp leaves and ran my knife through the flames in my fire.

Next, I drew a picture of the bunny in my journal.

November 12: Dear baby bunny, I'm sorry I couldn't save your life. Thank you for saving mine.

My food smelled really good. It was the best thing I'd eaten in weeks, but I cried while I ate it. I swore I could feel myself getting stronger, though. It was like my body was regenerating. Maybe I would live to see twelve after all.

22

I woke up freezing in the middle of the night, even though I was wearing pajamas, sweats, and my coat, and was under all the same blankets I used every night. I was so cold I couldn't sleep, and the harder I tried, the worse it got. My muscles ached from shivering. I was practically vibrating. I layered on more clothes and put my hat on under my hood. I piled on every blanket I had. Nothing seemed to work.

I considered dragging my tent over to the fire pit, but that would just mean keeping my tent open, and I was pretty sure more cold air would come in than heat. I hugged my legs and draped the heaviest cover over my whole body, hoping my breath would keep me warm.

Eventually, I uncovered myself and realized the sun had come out. Outside, everything was white with snow. I looked at the roof and Her Majesty's protruding branches. They were white, too. No wonder I was so cold. It was literally freezing outside.

If I stayed here, I was going to burn off all my calories shivering, and probably die of starvation and frostbite at the same time. I grabbed my journal and checked the last entry. Today was November thirteenth. Wasn't that early for it to be snowing?

"Who knows," I mumbled to myself. "It doesn't matter if it's early or not. It is what it is."

I had survived so far. It wasn't easy, but I had managed to stay alive. I didn't know the first thing about living through winter in the mountains, though. And even if I did, I probably didn't have what I needed to make it happen.

A growl escaped my throat. I was mad at the mountains, mad at Auntie Raven, mad at my family, mad at the weather, and *furious* at myself. I hated everything. This was all my fault. I didn't have to come stay with Auntie Raven. I had begged and pleaded. I didn't have to stay for school, either. When I realized it was because of me that my parents didn't come, I could have packed all the food and started walking to town or the nearest cabin. I knew how to pack, hike, and camp well enough to survive the couple of days it would probably take to get to town, even if I did get lost on the way.

But no. I stayed to keep myself out of trouble. I stayed to keep Mama and Auntie Raven from a permanent silent treatment. I had something to prove—something to accomplish. And look how it was ending up. I was going to look like the man at the end of that movie I wasn't supposed to watch in the first place, where he was frozen stiff, stuck in the snow. And it all happened because of *him*. In fact, his family left him there like that.

I zipped my tent shut and sat on the bed to think. I rocked back and forth while my mind raced. I wanted my real bed and a hot bath and my books and my friends. I wanted a normal birthday with chocolate overflow cake and candles and presents. I wanted a heater and a big, fat hamburger and a vanilla milkshake.

I wanted to go home.

I wrapped all the blankets around myself and laid down. I stayed there rocking myself for a long time. I hugged Pokey and thought about Arik.

"Pokey, I don't know what to do," I said.

Pokey stared at me. I could tell he was judging me.

"I know. I shouldn't give up."

No answer from Pokey.

"If I'm pretending to be Queen of the Wilderness, I guess I better figure out how to keep myself alive, huh?"

I made Pokey nod at me.

I was going to get in trouble, either now or later. Mama and Auntie Raven were going to have a big fight, either now or later. The timing didn't change the facts. I screwed up.

The decision was made. It wasn't really a decision, though, because if I wanted to live, I didn't have a choice. I had to walk to the nearest neighbors. I had to admit I needed help. This was the one thing I had to get right. When I got there, I could use their phone, stay warm, and maybe they'd share their dinner with me.

I'd never been to the neighbor's house. We'd never even passed it in the truck. So how would I get there? I packed my big camping backpack, bundled up, and sat on my bed. I closed my eyes and visualized Professor Young's 20-Mile Map. The one Auntie Raven thought was silly, because she had *knowledge and intuition*. Well, that wasn't going to be enough for me. I needed *details and help*.

Auntie's cabin was the center of the map. The neighbors were at the top end, which meant ten miles north. On a good day, I could walk about three miles in an hour. I had a feeling this was not going to be a good day, so it would probably take at least four hours to get there. It might take even longer because of the snow. Hopefully, I wouldn't pass out. We'd hiked enough for me to know which way was north. I tried to remember all the landmarks the professor had noted. The first was Her Majesty. The second was the clearing where I had my archery practice. I couldn't remember what came next, but I needed to head out now so I could use all the daylight. I'd think on the way. One thing was for sure: I couldn't afford to get lost.

My feet crunched in the snow as I headed slowly toward the clearing. At the clearing, I closed my eyes again and remembered a word. *Dead*. Dead what? Dead end? *Deadwood*. It was a tree. Professor Young had drawn it black, and taller than the rest, with no leaves. It was northwest of the clearing. A dirt road ran next to it. I had to get to the road.

My legs ached as I headed up the mountain. I had to stop to catch my breath twice before I got to the road. I was terrified that some weirdo would see me and offer a ride. That's how people went missing. But I put on the orange beanie from Alex and stayed right in the middle of the road. The sooner I got to the neighbors, the better.

I thought about Alex saying that the Black people always died first in wilderness movies because we didn't have any business being out there in the first place. "No comment," I said out loud.

I travelled uphill and watched my breath in the air. Every step was a struggle. It was more exercise than I'd had in weeks, and my muscles felt wobbly. A few times, I had to sit down. I listened to the forest. Even the birds were quieter than usual today, and I hadn't heard a single car. It was weird how weather so deadly could be beautiful and peaceful at the same time. On and on I walked, even though my body tried to convince me to give up.

There's another road. At first, I thought someone was behind me. Then I realized the voice was my brain whispering to me. *Knowledge and intuition.* I closed my eyes so I could see the map. Somewhere, another, narrower road veered off to the right. It wound up and to the right on the map. It led to the neighbors' cabin. And it was probably covered with snow.

As I stumbled along, watching for an opening in the trees wide enough to be a road, the sun was on its own journey across the sky. My chest hurt every time I inhaled, and the back of my throat tasted like blood. I ate a few small handfuls of snow to soothe it.

Eventually, I knew if I didn't eat, I'd collapse, so I sat down and ate my chips. It was all I had now that the garden was covered with snow. I knew better than to sit too long. I didn't want to get stiff or too cold. I sighed, stood up, and continued on. Every once in a while, I caught a glimpse of one of the high peaks. It looked like Mother Nature had draped a white blanket over it. It was beautiful, but it was also scary. Winter was coming early.

Finally, I found the road leading to the house. I remembered the map showing that it was nowhere near as long as the road I had just travelled, which was a good thing because I was running out of daylight. And energy. I followed the barely visible road, which was more like a path, for at least another hour. I noticed a large boulder and smiled. It was on the map, labeled *Boulder.* I was going the right way. As the sun sank, I saw the house in the distance, through the trees.

I made it.

I picked up my pace and knocked on the door. I realized I probably looked like somebody they didn't want to let in—dirty, skinny, and smelly. Mama's words about there not being any Black folks up here came to mind, too, and I hoped these people weren't racist. Nobody came to the door, so I knocked again.

When there was no response the second time,

I went over to the window to see if I could peek through the curtains. I couldn't.

"Hello?" I called, trying to sound chipper. "Anybody home?"

I walked around the corner of the house just in case the people were outside in the back. I noticed a piece of paper on a gigantic shed near the back of the house and went to look at it. It was soggy, but in big black letters, it said, "Dan, we had to leave town. We'll let you know when we get back."

"ARE YOU KIDDING ME?" I screamed. "They're not home?"

I mumbled a bunch of words Mama didn't allow me to say and stomped my foot like André. What I *wasn't* going to do was walk back home right now. I didn't come all this way for nothing. Obviously, Dan wasn't here, and I doubted he was showing up today, because it was almost dark.

I looked back at the house and turned in a slow circle to see if there was anyone else out here. I was the only idiot outside right now.

"Forget this," I said. "I'm breaking in."

23

I went up the three steps to the front door and wondered how much jail time I could get for breaking into somebody's house. There had to be exceptions for kids who might be about to die. I had my journal and wallet; maybe I could leave an apology note and all my cash. Would they forgive me? It wasn't like I was going to vandalize it. I would just sleep inside and maybe eat some of their food. And use their phone if they had one.

As I stood there wondering what the consequence would be for breaking in, I got colder. Much colder. I had to get inside. But what if Dan showed up? What if Dan was dangerous? Or what if he was a totally nice guy who had a gun and found an intruder?

To get in, I would have to break a window, and doing that would let in cold air. It couldn't be worse than being in a tent, though. And maybe I could go sleep in a bedroom. I tried the doorknob. Locked. I noticed a wooden statue of a bear that reminded me of Auntie Raven's loon statue. That was where Auntie Raven hid her keys. I tipped the bear sideways, but there was no key.

While I was standing there working up the nerve to throw another rock at a window, I heard a faint, high-pitched sound. It was so faint, I wasn't even sure if I really heard it. It came again, and this time I realized it was coming from beneath me. There was something under the porch. My heart thumped as I stood there frozen.

The third time I heard the sound, I realized it sounded like whining. Whatever was under the porch was an animal, and I was pretty sure it was crying. *Desperate animals attack*, I thought to myself. I fished my flashlight out of my backpack and put the whistle in my mouth. I held my knife in the other hand.

Under the stairs was hollow, and now I noticed

what looked like drips of blood in the snow. I backed up and aimed my light under there. I gasped. There were animals under there, but I couldn't tell what they were. They all looked dead, but one must be still alive. I got close enough see what they were. *Puppies.* Very young puppies. My heart sank and I had to work hard not to have another crying-vomiting breakdown.

Something had attacked them. But whatever had been here was gone now. I got on my hands and knees and peered in. There was no mama, and only one puppy was squirming. "Oh my god, you poor baby!" I whispered.

Grateful for my winter gloves, I held my breath and moved the dead puppies out of the way until I could reach the survivor. I pulled it out as carefully as I could in case it was injured. It didn't try to bite me or get away. It was trembling, and I didn't know if it was scared, or cold, or both. It whined again when I held it under my flashlight. It had all black fur and it was way too thin, but I didn't see any wounds.

Nature was cruel. That must have been where the phrase *survival of the fittest* came from. If you weren't either fit or lucky, you'd be dead. "We're in the same boat, puppy," I said. "But not for long."

I was trying to figure out how to break the window and climb through with the puppy when I had another idea. I should check the shed first. Maybe I wouldn't have to break into the house. If I could break into the shed and make it through the night, maybe the people would come back, and I could ask for help like a normal person instead of some kind of a juvenile delinquent.

I unzipped my jacket and tucked the puppy in there to keep it warm and free up my hands. Poor thing had to be freezing, especially with no body fat. *Maybe that's why I'm so cold*, I thought. On my way to the shed, I picked up a big rock to break the lock with. I shined the flashlight on the lock and smiled. Nature had been unkind to the lock, too. It was old and rusty, and I hoped that meant it would break easily. I banged on it with the rock. It took several hard hits, but the screws fell out of the wood and the entire thing came off.

I hurried in and shut the door. The shed was only slightly warmer than it was outside. I shined my light around. There were shelves going all the way around two sides, and the third side had stacks of plastic bins. The floor was concrete. I approached the first shelf and found two huge, battery powered lanterns. I turned them on and said, "Well, these people don't hate technology."

The shed was more like some kind of storm shelter. One shelf had batteries in every size imaginable, with flashlights, heaters, radios, and a boom box. Another shelf had two can openers and a bunch of canned food. My mouth watered reading the labels: raviolis, corn, chicken noodle soup, tuna, chicken, pork 'n' beans, green beans, spaghetti and meatballs. They even had canned milk, which I didn't know was a thing. Below that were packaged foods like crackers, cereal, peanut butter, jelly, honey, rice cakes, granola bars, and trail mix. On the bottom shelf, I found bottled water and juice. I felt stupid for not leaving my camp sooner. This place was a tiny Target.

Sitting on a little table was a burner that didn't have to be plugged in. Next to it was a pot and some dishes. There was a pile of blankets, a tent, sleeping bags, a roll up mattress, and just about anything else you could possibly want if you were stuck in a blizzard. One shelf even had books, games, and toys.

The puppy squirmed against my stomach and whined. I took it out of my coat and inspected it again. There was no blood at all, and it didn't act like being touched was painful. It blinked its eyes at me, and then closed them again. I put it on one of the blankets and it flopped down. Then I put a heater in each corner of the shed and turned them on. I did a little dance in the middle of the shed, and I didn't care if it was a sign I was losing my mind. If I died out here, it wasn't going to be tonight.

I would never bad-mouth modern conveniences again. There was a reason people invented them in the first place. Living like I had been living was definitely *not* convenient.

I wanted to feed the puppy first, so I opened the canned milk to warm it up. It was thick and sort of gooey and didn't taste like milk to me at all. I dumped it in the pot and added a little bit of water so the puppy wouldn't choke on it. While I waited for it to heat, I heard something shuffling outside the shed. At first, I was worried it was Dan. But then I heard a low snarl. It didn't sound big enough to be a bear, but it didn't sound small, either. It moved around the outside of the shed until it got to the door. It growled again and sniffed at the bottom of the door. I hoped it wasn't whatever killed the rest of the puppies. I also hoped it wasn't smart enough—or big enough—to push the door open.

24

I stood as still as possible, waiting to see if the animal would go away. It continued to sniff and growl, but didn't try to get in. The puppy whined and whatever was outside scratched at the door. I tiptoed to the door and leaned against it.

The puppy whined again and the thing outside let out a long howl. I'd had enough nighttime wild animal visitors to last me the rest of my life. There was nothing I could do to stop the puppy from whining. Plus, I was sure whatever was out there could smell us. I needed to either wait it out or scare it away. If I blew the whistle, I'd probably scare the poor puppy. If I waited it out, I might be standing here all night—and there was no way I was doing that. I would be eating and sleeping tonight.

Keeping my weight against the door, I got down as low as I could. I put my face at the doorjamb, took in as deep a breath as I could, and I *growled*. It was long, and low, and convincing. It was the growl of an animal who did not come to play. I even scared myself.

When I ran out of breath, I put my ear to the door. Whatever was out there sniffed one more time, then trotted away. Relieved and satisfied, I dragged four of the big bins in front of the door. I wasn't doing that again.

The milk had gotten too hot, so I spooned a little bit at a time, blew on it, tested it with my bottom lip, and then poured it into the puppy's mouth, just like Mama used to do when she fed the twins. The puppy had a good appetite and didn't seem to mind that it was canned milk. When it was full, it plopped back down on the blanket and went to sleep.

"Now *I* can finally eat!" I said.

I warmed up the raviolis and ate them straight out of the pot. Then I washed them down with a bottle of water. I was still hungry, so I popped open a can of chicken. After I ate, I made myself at home.

I used the roll up mattress, a thick winter sleeping bag, and blankets to make a bed. I went through the bins and found dog food, pillows, more blankets, and even some CDs.

I went through the CDs. The collection was all stuff I'd never heard of before. There were even some by Black musicians. I picked one by someone named Tracy Chapman and put it in the boom box next to my bed.

I didn't know how much I missed the sound of human voices until they started singing. It wasn't music I would have picked if I had a choice, but it was soothing. I watched the puppy sleep while I listened.

I realized I didn't know if it was a boy or a girl. I considered picking it up to check, but we had all been through enough for one day, so I left it alone. I wanted a name that was just right. I'd think of some, and then tomorrow I'd pick one.

I turned off one lamp and sat on my bed with my journal.

November 13: I almost lost it when I found out these people had left town, but today has been one of

the best. I have company, food, heat, and music. I won't
break into the house. I'll take as much as I can carry
back to my camp. Then I'll figure out how to get to
town.

I cuddled up under my blankets in the warm shed and smiled. I had probably saved the little motherless puppy's life.

My thoughts turned to my own mother. I wondered what she was doing. Maybe she was wrapped in a blanket listening to music, too. Deep down, I'd been mad at her for a long time about Auntie Raven. Now I understood what it felt like to have one of the people you love most just up and leave.

I understood Auntie Raven, too. I wanted to live in the wilderness one day. Just like her—or maybe *with* her. In a cabin with some modern conveniences next time, but still, I loved it here. And now that I had rescued the puppy, I knew why she did what she did. I didn't want the puppy to die alone, so I saved it. It was the exact same thing she did for Professor Young and for Sophia. It was what good people did. It was what lonely people did, too.

Mama and her sister needed to sit down and talk.

They were hurting themselves and me. I had failed at fixing things, so they'd have to do it themselves.

I pushed them out of my mind. I didn't feel like crying tonight. For one night, I just wanted to fall asleep happy. I looked at the puppy again. It was adorable.

"Good night, puppy," I whispered.

It lifted its chin and gave me one wag of its tail, and that was all I needed . . . for tonight.

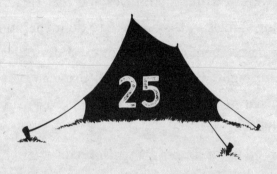

25

I woke up to the puppy licking my face. "Good morning," I said.

It whined, and I knew it wanted to eat. I wasn't sure if it was my imagination, but the puppy already looked like it had gained weight. I made a new pot of milk, and while it heated, I lifted the puppy and checked its privates. It was a girl. That didn't mean it needed a girly name, though. I'd have to give it some thought. I fed her and then she licked my fingers and went right back to sleep. I loved her already.

While I ate granola bars and canned pineapple, I thought about how unpredictable the Adirondack Mountains were. The tree falling, the raccoon fight, the hole in my tent, being abandoned up here like a lost puppy . . . and now things were looking up.

"I know!" I said. "Let's name you Ronnie! After the Adirondacks. Get it? That's a good name!"

Ronnie wagged her tail, so it was settled. Now I had things to do. I needed to get back to the cabin, so I could plan my trip to town. And I knew enough to start back early, so I wouldn't be walking around in the dark. I emptied a bin that had good handles and packed it with food for myself and Ronnie, along with water, two heaters, a lantern, the burner, and the pot. I put as much as I could in my backpack and then strapped the sleeping bag to it. I found a rope and tied a tent to the bin and then to the handle so I could pull everything. I cleaned up behind myself, and then I sat down to write the people a note.

Dear neighbors,

I'm so sorry I broke into your shed and stole your things. I'm stranded in the mountains alone with no food or shelter. I came for help, but you were gone. Please don't call the police on me. I'm just a kid.

I left you all my money, but I know it's not enough. I will pay you back as soon as I can. I will bring back your appliances, too. You can also call my parents. I'll put their number at the bottom of this note. Please don't be too mad at me.

Thank you,

Ava

PS—My auntie is Raven, your neighbor.

I put the note and the money on the table where the burner had been. I was sad to leave the shed, but it was the only choice. I couldn't wait around for someone to show up. I already knew that didn't work out very well for me. Plus, for all I knew, Dan had come by, seen the note, and had no plan to come back until the people called him like they said they would.

I kneeled in front of Ronnie. "You need to come with me. I'll feed you and keep you warm, okay?"

She wagged her tail, and I picked her up.

"Awww, hi, Ronnie," I said. "You are so cute! I love you." I kissed her nose and she licked mine.

She looked at me like she was saying thank you. I kissed her little forehead and hugged her. I put everything outside the shed and did my best to make it so the door would stay closed. I got a few small sticks and wedged them under the crack below the door so it wouldn't swing open.

I grabbed everything, being careful not to squish Ronnie in my jacket, and looked at the shed one last time. It had saved my life. And if I could get here, I could get to town, because even though town wasn't on Professor Young's map, I had food and water. It would take longer, but I had made up my mind. Nothing could stop me. And since Auntie Raven's was on the way, I had a safe spot to stop, rest, and get organized. I'd eat, get some sleep, and hopefully feel strong enough to head to town tomorrow. I pulled the bin toward the little road, back the same way I had come. My feet kept sinking into the snow, which I now realized was deeper, and the bin bounced around behind me. I cradled

Ronnie with one hand. For the first time in a while, I felt hopeful. I was rested and full, and I had what I needed to stay alive and well for at least a week. Hopefully, everything would be easier from now on.

It started snowing again, and a beautiful silence settled into the forest and into my spirit. The closer I got to Auntie Raven's, the more I relaxed, and I finally slowed my pace. It was much easier going downhill and not having an empty stomach, so I made good progress, despite the fact that it was colder than yesterday. It was weird how relieved I felt when I caught the first glimpse of "home," even though it wasn't much of one. Especially compared to the shed.

"Welcome to my house, Ronnie," I said.

She looked up at me like she was confused. I laughed because even a dog could see I wasn't living right.

In front of the cabin, I paused. There were paw prints all over the ground. *Big* paw prints. I kneeled down and examined them. A bear had been here. I looked toward my tent. The tarp was halfway off, and one side of the tent was shredded. My heart pounded. My eyes darted around to make sure the bear wasn't sitting around waiting for me. *Bears don't do that, Ava,* I thought.

"But they do come back," I said out loud.

I left everything where it was and approached the tent. I didn't know why a bear would come here anyway. There was literally no food. That's part of why I left in the first place. It didn't look like the bear had been inside the tent. Maybe it recognized a place where people would be and assumed there was food and then left when there wasn't any. I knew they would be trying to gain weight right now so they could hibernate.

"Stupid bear," I told Ronnie. "I thought they were smarter than that."

One thing was for sure. I had to figure out how to stay safe. Now there *was* food. And a puppy to protect. And weather too cold for a tent. I knew what I had to do. I had to move into the rickety shed. At least for tonight. It wasn't even big enough to park a car in, but it was better than sleeping outside. I remembered Auntie Raven's warning: *Wait out here, Ava. I don't trust this shed not to cave in.*

I set up the borrowed tent, turned the laundry

basket on its side, and lined it with the smallest blanket. I put Ronnie inside. Then I got to work. *Fast*.

I opened the shed door carefully and stepped all the way inside. It was too full for me to even make a bed on the floor, so I started taking things out. There were tools, a container of gas, a bunch of broken stuff, and a stack of bins labeled *Byron's Belongings*. There was one bin that said *Emergency*. I opened that one and found corroded batteries, a tiny radio, two lighters, extra men's clothes, and a few cans of beans so old they looked like they were from colonial times.

At the bottom there was a store-bought fire log. "Really?" I said. "*After* I chopped off my hair?" I growled and threw it as far as I could. Then I went and got it and put it back in the bin with the other useless junk.

As I cleared the shed, I stacked bins around the perimeter to reinforce it, keeping the one with the beans on the bottom of the stack so the bear wouldn't find it. I kept an eye on Ronnie, who was fast asleep. I used an old broom to get down the spiderwebs and squish a few big spiders, swept the floor, and brought in a lantern.

Now I inspected my temporary home. There were no holes in the roof, but the back wall definitely looked rotten. The top board was sagging, like it was about to break under the pressure of the roof. I had no desire to be under a falling roof again. I'd have to rig it somehow.

I remembered the big wooden boards Auntie Raven had stacked on the garden side of the house. We were supposed to use them for the shed, but she left. I ran to get them, but I was afraid to hammer anything to the decaying walls. They looked like they could collapse at any moment. Instead, I wedged the boards from the floor to the ceiling, hoping that reinforcing the wall that way would hold the shed up. I did the same thing outside, so the bad wall was being held up on both sides. Then I put extra boards outside at an angle that would add extra support.

I was hungry again, but I knew I couldn't stop to eat before I finished. I brought my stolen bin inside, set up my bed against the wall, and moved the things I needed from my tent to the shed. I brought the puppy inside, too. The last thing I did was put the bow and arrows against the wall near the door. If that bear came back, I was not going down without a fight. I had come too far to die now.

When Ronnie and I finally sat down outside for dinner, I realized how sweaty I had gotten. Being damp was making me colder now that I was sitting still. After we were nice and full, I decided to hunker down in the shed until bedtime. But first, I dragged the metal garbage can as far away from my camp as possible. I tossed the empty cans in and wrapped the bungee cord around it extra tight. Then I used snow to rinse the dishes. *I'm not giving that bear a reason to come back*, I thought.

"Ronnie, it's too cold out here," I said. "We have to stay in."

And that's exactly what we did. Ronnie didn't seem to mind at all. We only went out to go to the bathroom, and I spent the rest of the time writing in my journal, sketching pictures of Ronnie and the shed, and being grateful for food, heat, and light.

Before I went to sleep, I sang the Winnie the Pooh song to Ronnie. As I fell asleep, I thought about my trip to town. And going home. And my birthday.

26

In the middle of the night, I woke up in a full sweat. I wondered if the heaters were over-heating and turned one off. I probably needed to save some of the battery power anyway. I tried to go to back to sleep, but I couldn't cool off. I tried laying on top of the covers, which I knew was dumb, because it was freezing outside. I tossed and turned so much that Ronnie lifted her head, stared at me sadly, and then gave me a little kiss. Finally, I turned off the second heater, drank a bunch of water, and managed to doze back off.

When I woke up again, my shirt was soaked. I took it off, but before I could put a new one on, I noticed my arm. Until now, the stupid tick hanging out in my arm hadn't given me any problems. Now the area around it was red, and it reminded me of the bull's-eye targets Auntie Raven had hung up the day she taught me to use a bow and arrows.

"Oh no, Ronnie," I said. "I have an infection or something."

She cocked her head at me. She was trembling. I was hot and she was freezing. *Do I have a fever?* I wondered. I turned the heaters back on.

"Or . . . Lyme disease," I said. I stared at my arm and hoped I wasn't hosting a deer tick. I was so excited about all the stuff in the neighbor's shed, I hadn't thought about a first aid kit at all. Now I regretted it.

Suddenly, I jumped up, remembering the Tylenol. That's what Mama gave me when I had a fever at home. I took one and hoped it would kick in soon. Meanwhile, I fed Ronnie and ate some soup. I had to make myself feel better.

I burst into tears. If I couldn't get the fever down, I would never make it to town. The trip would take at least two days, and I'd have to sleep in the tent. My birthday was only four days away. If I didn't get to town, not only was I going to be by myself with no celebration, I'd run out of food and have to go back to the neighbors' house. I would literally be going backward. Ronnie whined at me. At first, I thought she felt sorry for me, but she was hungry again.

"Thanks for the sympathy," I said, wiping my eyes.

After I fed Ronnie, I looked at my arm. Besides being red and swollen, a yellowish fluid was oozing out. I could *not* let this stop me. I took out the lighter and my knife. First, I ran the flame up and down the blade on each side to disinfect it. Then I held the flashlight in my mouth, aimed at my arm. I found the center of my wound, where there was a small, black spot. The tick. I knew performing this little surgery on myself might backfire, but leaving the tick in for too long, especially now that it was making me sick, was a bad idea. I certainly wasn't about to let it kill me.

I held my breath and bit my lower lip so I wouldn't scream, stuck the tip of my knife into my skin, and wedged it under the tick. Blood and fluid oozed out. I kept the knife in my skin, under the tick, and moved it in a tiny circle, carving the tick out. It was like taking out a splinter by removing the skin it was in. And it hurt.

With a final upward motion of the tip of the blade, I pulled the little chunk of skin off my arm. It smelled rotten and I let out a little whimper-scream. I had left behind a small hole, but not the tick. I wiped it on the shirt I had taken off, balled it up as tight as possible, and stuck it inside the bear canister. I hoped it would stay trapped in there. Then I got a clean pair of underwear and pressed them against the wound to stop the bleeding.

The Tylenol hadn't started working yet, so I laid down, holding my arm. I wasn't going to be able to leave for town today. Between the fever and the pain in my arm, I knew I wouldn't make it. Ronnie cuddled up against my neck, and we both went to sleep.

For the next two days, all I could do was feed myself and Ronnie, and sleep. Removing the tick hadn't taken away the infection. I alternated between freezing and sweating, and whether I was hot or cold, I had the chills. Ronnie stuck right by my side, giving me kisses. It was like she knew something was wrong. I had to get out of this shed. I had to get to town. I wanted my Mama.

On the third day, I decided to do something I had seen Mama do. Usually, she only took one Tylenol, but every now and then, if she had a really bad headache, she took two. I ate my breakfast and then took the two pills with a lot of water. And I didn't wait to see if it would work. We needed to leave. On top of everything else, Ronnie and I were running low on food.

I moved the security board I had pushed through the handle in case a bear tried to come in, but when I pushed on the door, it didn't move. I tried again with no luck. I leaned against it with all my weight, but it didn't budge. Ronnie looked up at me.

"It won't open!" I told her.

Then my fever-damaged brain figured it out. We were snowed in. That was the only explanation. The snow had piled up against the door and blocked it. "Oh no. No, no, no. This can't be happening," I muttered. "We need to get out. We need food. I want to go home."

For one delusional second, I hoped the snow

would melt, but that didn't make any sense. That much snow wasn't going to melt in a few hours . . . or a few days.

I looked at Ronnie, who was standing up on her blanket. While I'd been busy deteriorating, she'd perked up and was almost pudgy now. She wagged her tail. Then she went over to the corner of the shed and peed.

When was the last time I went to the bathroom? I wasn't sure, but it had been at least since yesterday. I was dehydrated. My lips were extra chapped, too. I fetched the lip balm I had thrown to the side when I got the Tylenol. I wondered how much worse things would get, since I was obviously going to have all the bad luck available.

What would Auntie Raven do?

"Auntie Raven would never be in this situation in the first place," I told myself.

I laid on my stomach with my journal, while Ronnie kept trying to bite my pen.

November 18: Today is my birthday's eve, if that's a word, and it sucks. I think I have an infection from this stupid tick I had to cut out of my own arm, and I have a fever, and my food is almost gone, and I'm snowed in. I have no idea how deep the snow is. Hopefully, we aren't buried alive. I hope being snowed in doesn't mean anyone coming this way is snowed OUT.

I WANT TO GO HOME.

I'm not dying up here and neither is my dog. Since tomorrow is my birthday, I'm throwing myself a party. I'm going to raise the roof. Literally. I'm busting out of here.

I had made up my mind. Tomorrow, I was leaving here. I had to get to town. I needed help. And medical attention. I didn't know how to survive out here. I couldn't do it alone, and it wasn't even the worst part of winter yet.

"Tomorrow, we leave," I told Ronnie. She put her paw on my hand. We had just made a pact.

That night, Ronnie burrowed into my sleeping bag with me. I laid awake thinking about tomorrow, and what I should take with me. Probably not much. I would put our necessities in the bin and cover it with blankets. Then Ronnie could ride on the top. I'd bring the camping backpack, the tent, and a change of clothes . . . and the bow and arrows.

I was dozing off when I heard leaves crunching outside, like somebody was walking around out there. Ronnie and I sat still. My instincts were screaming *Bear!* Sticks snapped under its weight. I grabbed Ronnie and held her close. I double-checked that I had put my security board back across the door and luckily, I had.

There was a crash that sounded like one of the bins outside the shed falling over, then a rummaging sound. Another crash followed. I was positive there was a bear out there, and it was looking for something to eat. A third bin fell over, then there was a long silence, followed by more leaves crunching. The bear went toward the back of the shed . . . where the weakest wall was. I imagined its claws tearing through the rotten wood.

Then the bear sounded like it was leaving. The footsteps and crunching sounds got farther and farther away until I didn't hear them at all. I didn't move, though. I had no desire to investigate. I would stay my behind right inside this shed until tomorrow, and when I broke out of the roof, I'd be aiming an arrow.

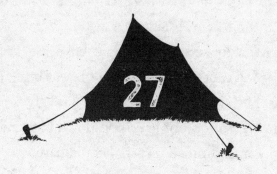

27

I woke up to brighter-than-usual light shining in between two of the boards. I must have slept late after such a rough night. We had made it through the night, though, which was apparently my birthday present. I fed Ronnie immediately, then ate my last two granola bars with two more Tylenol. Then I prepared to bust us out of the shed. If I was stuck in a shed, I'd never be found. I *had* to get out. My life depended on it.

I carefully removed one of the support boards and stood under the center of the roof, which was only four or five feet above my head. I gripped it as tightly as I could and rammed it into the roof. It punctured a hole in the wood and snow fell on me. The roof was weaker than I expected. I put my head down to keep stuff out of my eyes and rammed the board through the roof over and over again.

Finally, I looked up. The light hurt my eyes and they needed time to adjust. The hole was big enough for the bin to fit through, so I stopped. I stacked the big suitcase on top of the upside-down bin, grabbed an arrow, and climbed on top. I could barely see out, so I hoisted myself up.

There was no bear waiting to kill me, but there was a lot of snow. It came halfway up the shed, and covered what was left of the roof. I was lucky it hadn't caved in on me. I'd have to be careful climbing out, too, so I didn't fall right back through the roof.

I started throwing things out of the shed, like I had when I looted Auntie Raven's bedroom. Bow and arrows. Backpack with necessities. Blankets and warm clothes. Canned milk, water, and a can of beans.

"I think that's it," I told Ronnie. "Now it's your turn."

I tied one end of the rope around the bin and the other around my waist. Then I bundled up, put Ronnie in my coat, and climbed on top for the last time. I pulled the bin to the roof with the rope and threw it to the ground so I could put everything back in it.

I sat on the shed roof and half slid, half jumped to the ground. My feet sank into the snow and my legs followed until the snow was up to my knees. It was too deep and much too soft to support the weight of a full bin. I would just have to leave it there. I set off toward town with everything I could fit inside my backpack and Ronnie in my coat. I put her body against mine but left her head out so she could see. My arm throbbed, and I was in a full sweat before I got to the end of the driveway, but it didn't matter. I was finally leaving.

Every step was a struggle, because I kept sinking. I stayed in the middle of the road so I could be discovered by anyone who drove by. But at this pace, it would take me a week to get to town. And I didn't have a week. I realized the trees at the side of the road had sheltered the ground from some of the snow, so I made my way over there. I thought it would be easier to walk, and I smiled when I learned I was right.

I struggled through the snow for what felt like hours, but had still only managed to make it just past the mailbox. I was exhausted and I was starting to feel faint. My fever was spiking again. I needed to rest. I didn't have a choice. I leaned against a tree and let myself slide to the ground. I rested my head on the trunk and closed my eyes. I could feel myself falling asleep, but I couldn't stop it no matter how hard I tried. My eyes closed.

Two things woke me up. Ronnie licking my nose and a sound. It was the sound of an engine! It was still in the distance, but it was slowly getting closer. Maybe I could flag it down. I tried to stand up, but didn't have the strength. The engine crept closer. It crossed my mind that it might be the police coming to arrest me for robbing Auntie Raven's neighbors, but that was a chance I had to take. I needed help. Even police would be able to see that.

I kept trying to get up, but my legs were stiff and I didn't have any energy. Ronnie whined and licked the tears as they rolled down my cheeks. Poor Ronnie. If I didn't get help, neither would she. I dug the whistle from my pocket, put it in my mouth, and pushed Ronnie down into my coat and zipped her in.

I crawled toward the sound of the engine. Eventually, I could see it was a gigantic snowplow. It looked like something only a park ranger would drive.

Three people sat in the front. None of them were dressed like police officers. The driver had on a fur cap and a puffy coat. The person in the middle was smaller and wore a black winter coat with the hood on. They had pulled the drawstring so tight that only the center of their face peeked out. The person in the passenger seat wore something I recognized immediately. A beanie with a high school logo. *Daddy's* high school.

I sat in the snow and blew the whistle. I blew over and over and over again until the snowplow slowed down.

Mama climbed over Daddy and jumped out while they were still rolling. She fell to the ground and grabbed me. "Oh, baby! I'm so glad you're okay!" She held me at arm's length. "You are okay, right?"

I hugged Mama and buried my face in her coat. We kneeled in the snow hugging and crying. I wasn't okay, but I would be. She held me away from her and wiped my tears away. Then she hugged me again. "It's going to be okay, honey. You're safe now."

Daddy fell to his knees next to us and took me in his arms. "Thank God," he said. Then his whole body shook as he sobbed. "Thank God," he repeated, squeezing me so tight that Ronnie whined.

In this moment, I knew one thing for sure. No matter how mad they were after I told them everything, they would still love me. They would always love me. And I would always love them.

We let go of each other, and I pulled Ronnie out of my coat. My parents didn't say a word. The park ranger had joined us at the side of the road, so I handed Ronnie to him. He took her, and seeing that we needed a minute to ourselves, went back to the snowplow.

Without asking any questions, and without making any accusations or scolding me or acting disappointed, Mama and Daddy pulled me to my feet. Daddy picked me up like I was Arik or André and carried me to the snowplow. Mama walked next to us and rubbed my back. And I clung to my Daddy like I never had before.

We piled into the snowplow and the ranger turned back toward town. From Daddy's lap, I searched Mama's face for any signs that she was mad at me. There were none.

"Did the people call you?" I asked.

Daddy frowned. "The people?"

Now anger flashed across Mama's face. "Your *Auntie Raven* called us," Mama said with an attitude. "She called to tell you Happy Birthday, and to see if her present arrived."

Daddy put an arm on her shoulder. "Don't start," he said. "She's fine."

I was trying to keep up with what was going on. My parents arriving had nothing to do with the neighbors calling? Nothing to do with the note I left in their shed?

Mama opened her mouth, but Daddy put his hand on her arm. "We didn't know Raven left," he explained. "The email never came through."

"Apparently, there was a typo in the email address." Mama rolled her eyes.

"We came right away," Daddy added.

We sat in silence. I had a truth to tell, but now wasn't the time. This was a conversation we shouldn't have in front of the ranger. And I wanted a little more time to sit too close to my parents in peace before it all fell apart again.

"Ava, what happened?" asked Daddy. "Why were you on the side of the road?"

I told them the whole story, from arriving, to Auntie Raven leaving, to wondering if they were trying to teach me a lesson, to thinking they were dead, to the tree falling and trying to stay alive, to robbing the neighbors. They all looked shocked, especially the ranger.

"Most people wouldn't have survived all that," he said. "You bustin' out of that shed saved your life. We never would have found you."

"But what I don't understand," said Daddy, "is why you didn't come down the hill right away."

My parents looked at me. They were waiting for an answer.

"Can we talk about the rest of it later? Please?" I asked.

Mama nodded, and I leaned back against Daddy's chest and closed my eyes. With Mama's hand wrapped around mine and Daddy's heart beating in my ear, I dozed off.

When we got to town, Mama looked at Ronnie, who wagged her tail and looked like she was smiling. "Ava, you know we can't keep a dog at the apartment, right?"

"Mama, she's all alone," I said.

Daddy interrupted. "How about we keep her until we figure out where she can live?"

Mama sighed and walked into the library, where my brothers were waiting for us. The twins hugged my waist. When the hug was finally over, I looked at Alex. He was *crying*. He opened his arms and said, "Bring it in."

He gave me a bear hug and whispered, "I missed you. I'm glad you're okay." Then he pushed me away and said, "Ooo wee! You're funky. You smell like the locker room."

I laughed and said, "Shut up. And I missed you, too. Thanks for the snacks." I was starting to sweat again, and now that we were inside, I took off my hood and hat.

"Aw, dang!" yelled Alex. "What happened to your hair?"

I didn't even care that Alex went right back to being Alex. I would have been worried if he hadn't.

"Be quiet, Alex," said Daddy.

Mama's eyes practically popped out of her head, but she didn't say anything. The twins stared at my head.

"I cut it off," I explained. "All my firewood and kindling were wet, so I burned some of my hair to start a fire."

Alex looked at his fancy basketball shoes for a while. Then he said, "I would have died. For real. I don't even know how to cook my own food in a regular kitchen."

I couldn't believe the respect he was giving me. I had proven something after all.

"Ava, you're sweating," said Mama. She put her hand on my forehead. "You're burning up. Are you sick?"

I didn't feel good at all. "I have an infection. From a tick. I cut it out with my knife, but I need to go to the doctor."

Mama went into hysterics about the tick, while Daddy tried to calm her down. Arik and André begged to see it, and Alex said, "Dang, you cut a tick out of your own arm? You're kinda bad, huh?"

We were so loud, a lady in the corner stared at us and didn't look away until we quieted down.

"Let's get to the inn," said Mama. "I'll look at your arm, and you can get cleaned up."

While we checked in and settled into our room, Daddy said he needed to go pick up a couple of things. I took two Tylenol, stood in the shower until my skin was wrinkled, and then I put on the hotel robe.

Mama examined my arm. "It's definitely infected. I think we better leave it alone until tomorrow and keep an eye on your fever for now. I don't know anything about ticks. I can fix your hair, though."

Mama cut all the braids to the same short length, then unbraided them. She put a bunch of oils and curl-defining conditioner in my hair. It actually didn't look that bad. Daddy came in with presents and some touristy-looking pink Adirondack Park sweats and a subzero-weather coat for me.

Arik shouted, "Party tiiiiiime!"

My family took me out for a hamburger and a vanilla shake. Daddy had stopped somewhere and gotten me a chocolate overflow cake. He'd also gone to the post office and picked up the present they sent me. It was a box full of snacks, books, puzzles, and games. They brought the gift from Auntie Raven, which they had found in the lobby on their way out this morning. It was my very own bow and arrows. Arik and André got me earmuffs. They would have been perfect if I was staying.

Alex grinned and handed me a present. "I got you something, too."

Inside of a small box was a gift card for the Burger Joint. I smiled and stuck my tongue out at him.

"I tried to tell you Black folks don't have any business in the wilderness," said Alex, shaking his head.

Daddy frowned. "Ava has the blood of the ancestors flowing through her veins. She survived *because* she's Black. That's what we do."

It wasn't supposed to be funny, but I laughed. Not one thing had changed while I was gone. And I was glad. Because all the love was still there.

Alex and Daddy were right. "I'm not *kinda* bad," I said. "I'm all the way bad. I'm the Queen of the Wilderness!"

Alex shook his head at me, but he was smiling.

"And I'll do it again next time, too," I said. "You'll see."

29

I was glad to be back with my family, and I was grateful for the birthday celebration, but there was still one thing I needed to do: Tell the truth.

When we got back to our room and André, Arik, and Alex were happily watching TV on the bed, I asked Mama and Daddy if we could talk. We all sat on the other bed together.

"Daddy," I said, "remember how you asked why I didn't try to get help sooner?"

He nodded and Mama clenched her jaw. "I still can't believe Raven didn't have the sense to make sure we were coming. She can't even get a darn email right," said Mama.

"No, Mama. This was all my fault," I admitted.

"I got mad at Auntie Raven. I saw the typo when we were at the library, and I didn't say anything."

"What?" said Mama. "Why?"

I looked down. "I didn't know what the email was about. And I was mad at her. I figured whatever it was, she could just email you again next time if she didn't catch her mistake. Then she told me she had to leave and I had to go back home and I got upset and totally forgot about it. Until two weeks after you didn't show up."

Alex's eyes got big and he mouthed, "YOU ARE ABOUT TO GET IT."

Mama said, "You were mad at your auntie, so you let her think she sent an email?"

I nodded. "I shouldn't have held a grudge. I was wrong."

My parents were quiet for a long time. Finally, Daddy said, "That doesn't explain why you didn't get help after you realized what happened."

"At first, I wanted to prove I could survive. I wanted to make it all okay." I broke into tears. "I thought if I stayed until Christmas and was just fine, nobody would be mad at anybody. But then everything went wrong, and I was weak and I got scared. It felt like I might die whether I stayed or left."

Mama frowned. "You did this so we *wouldn't* be mad at you?"

"I did it so you wouldn't be mad at Auntie Raven anymore!" I said through tears. "I thought I could make you see the wilderness wasn't so bad. I thought you'd be grateful for everything she taught me. That everything was okay. And I was going to get straight As and make you proud."

"My problems with your auntie are *my* problems," said Mama. "And what you did was just as bad as what she does. Always doing whatever she wants without thinking about anyone else."

Daddy put a hand on Mama's shoulder and shook his head at her. But it was too late.

I stood up. Tears and snot ran down my face. "No, they're my problems, too. Because I don't get to have an auntie. And yeah, I'm just like her. Misunderstood and lonely and not accepted for who I am. Now you can hold a grudge against me, too. Give me the silent treatment. Have you ever thought about how *you* make *us* feel?"

Ronnie whined from her box in the corner. Mama opened her mouth and closed it again. I got Pokey out of my backpack and climbed in the bed next to Arik. He smiled and kissed us both. Alex stared at me, bug-eyed. Then he got up, walked around to my side of the bed, and hugged me.

"I'm sorry," he said.

I hugged him back and cried.

I felt Arik's little hand patting my back. "I love you, Ava. I'm going to be just like you when I grow up."

I looked at my parents. "I'm sorry. It was all my fault."

Mama looked at me and then looked down. "This is all my fault. And Auntie Raven's fault. You're a child trying to fix grown-up problems. You shouldn't have to do that."

Mama's cell phone rang and Daddy answered it. "Hi, Raven . . . Yeah, she'll be okay . . . No, this probably isn't a good time . . ."

Mama took the phone from Daddy. "Hello?"

She was quiet for a long time. I wished I could hear what Auntie Raven was saying. We all stared at her, waiting for the argument to start. Finally, she said, "I should have supported what you wanted to do."

Mama's voice was quiet and full of guilt. She had listened to what I'd said. It was the first time I'd ever spoken to her like that, and I was glad I had gone off.

She listened to whatever Auntie Raven was saying, and nodded like Auntie Raven could see her. "I just miss you so much," said Mama. "You're my best friend . . . I know . . . Oh, Raven, I love you, too . . . Maybe I'll take you up on that. See what it is you and Ava love so much . . . I'll have her call you tomorrow . . . Raven, I'm sorry to tell you this, but a big tree fell on it."

Mama went silent again. "Don't cry, Raven. It's going to be okay. You have a *family*," she said. Then she looked at me. "You also have a new puppy. Her name is Ronnie. Ava rescued her from the storm. You have to keep her, and Ava can come visit you both."

I smiled at Mama. I loved her more than I ever had. It was the perfect solution. She listened a while longer and chuckled. "She sure does have your knowledge and intuition." Then Mama got off the phone and stood by our bed. We all scooted over to make room for her. She took me in her arms, and I felt my body relax into hers. She stroked my hair and I felt myself falling asleep.

The last thing I heard was her whispering in my ear. "I love you."

ACKNOWLEDGMENTS

My journey into and through *Stranded* mirrors Ava's journey in so many ways, and at every twist and turn people have been there for me. Like Ava, I was born into a family full of love. My parents told me I could be anything I wanted to be, and one of those things was a Camp Fire Girl. So, I thank my mama and daddy, and all the people who made me feel like I belonged at Camp Okizu every year—in the lake, on the trails, tending fires, singing folk songs; I felt welcomed, always.

Writing a book is not as easy as being a Camp Fire Girl hiking to Gypsy Falls while belting out songs and yelling, "Car!" whenever we needed to move to the side of the road. But I had a trail family as I worked on this book. Thank you to my critique partners for dealing with my frenzies and silence. Take 10 sisters, thanks for the sprints and Zoom meetings, the texts, memes, and reels, for the friendship and the healing and all the things. To The Brown Bookshelf and Amplify Black Stories cohort . . . my community, my village, my fam . . . thank you.

I went through a period when I was stranded emotionally and in need of something I couldn't identify. The wise and beautiful students in my fourth-grade class at Fred T. Korematsu Elementary School (2021–2022) reminded me to dream and step outside of my comfort zone and encouraged (forced) me to take a poetry class on Cape Cod. I listened to them, and it changed my life. Because of them and the folks from my poetry class, I am brave, like Ava. Thank you all. Some of the words in this book were inspired by, and crafted at, the Highlights Foundation campus, surrounded by beautiful scenery and beautiful people, and fueled by good food— thank you for the nourishment.

This book was ushered into the world by a dream team: my agent, Jennifer March Soloway; my editors, Maya Marlette and Sam Palazzi, aka Ma'am; the folks at Scholastic who have handled more details than I can list. Special thanks to the designer, Cassy Price, and Juan Carlos Ribas, for the gorgeous cover.

My husband and children have watched me struggle, falter, question, hustle, procrastinate, dance, cry, pull all-nighters, disappear into distant lands (both literal and figurative), and dream. You have been by my side every step of the way. I appreciate you. I see you. I love you. Haley and Jesse, thank you for the monumental hike to the top of the Okolehao Trail on Kauai. You accompanied me on the last leg of my journey to myself. Babies, I love you forever.

Sometimes, confidence is elusive, but there are people in my life who see things in me I don't always see in myself. Thank you for the flashlight.

Readers, thank you for joining me on this journey. May you always have people around you who pull you out when you are stranded.

ABOUT THE AUTHOR

Nikki Shannon Smith was born and raised in Oakland, California, where she grew to love both the city and nature. She now lives in Woodland, California, but disappears onto beaches and hiking trails whenever she can. Nikki has worked in elementary education for more than thirty years and is the author of twenty books, ranging from board books to young adult novels. Find her online at nikkishannonsmith.com.